OPHELIA FEY

Saltblood

Daughter of the Brine

For my mother and father,
who gave me roots deep enough to hold in two worlds.
For my son,
who reminds me what the future is worth.
And for my past—
I didn't outrun you.
I made you into something I could carry.

"Cattle die, kinsmen die,
You yourself will also die;
But the word about you will never die,
If you win a good reputation."

— Poetic Edda, Hávamál, stanza
76

Contents

Foreword

Some of us are born with a natural awareness, long before we understand words. I understood feelings—places that felt heavier than they appeared, dreams that lingered beyond sleep, and a quiet knowing that pressed through the silence like breath through fog. I grew up in that space, surrounded by spiritual things that needed no proof, drawn to silence the way others are drawn to light.

This story didn't begin with writing. It started the way most true things do: quietly, in fragments. A name I'd never heard before. A presence that felt familiar—not imagined, but remembered.

I've always felt older than my years, not in body but in memory. I'm drawn to ancient stones, the sea, and names that echo even when no one speaks them. My roots trace back to the Channel Islands—wind-worn, coastal places where the past never fully lets go. That pull has shaped me, and this story is how I responded to it.

Saltblood is a work of fiction, but every word is rooted in something real—something felt, even if unseen. If you find pieces of yourself here, it may not be by chance.

Some things we inherit. Some things remind us. And some things… wait.

—Ophelia Fey

Preface

Before the world was carved into kingdoms and names, only the elements existed: stone, sea, blood, and breath. And in the hush between tides, something spoke. It was not a god, nor a devil. It was a hunger.

It slipped through the cracks of waking thought, drifted up from the deep trenches of the sea, and coiled itself around the hearts of those who lived closest to the water. Island women—barefoot, brine-marked, sleepless beneath moonlight—were the first to hear it. The cliffs echoed with waves, and in the silence that followed, the voice whispered not into their ears, but into the marrow of their bones.

Called from the deep, salted, and ancient, it awakened those who listened. Their dreams soured into visions. Their bodies remembered things they had never lived. And behind their eyes, something began to watch.

It spoke in runes and reflections, in the taste of metal and the pull of tides. Some claimed it was the sea itself—lonely, vast, alive. Others called it a remnant, a breath left behind by whatever came before the gods.

The Channel Islands bore the gateway. The Norwegian Sea held its echo. And the Isle of Man wore its seal: a triskelion spun in flesh, carved not by hand, but grown beneath the skin. Always watching and always waiting.

Some say those marked by the spiral were chosen to guard

the old ways. Others say they were never guardians at all—just vessels—soft, starlit bodies made for possession, bridges between blood, salt, and shadow.

But no matter what you believe, the truth remains.

When it calls your name, your reflection won't be the one who answers.

And what touches you from the other side... remembers everything.

Acknowledgments

This book would not exist without the people who helped carry it forward, especially in the moments when I wasn't sure I could.

To my mother and father, Art and Sue: Thank you for believing in me long before I learned how to believe in myself. You've given me a deep-rooted sense of place, history, and quiet resilience. I will never stop being shaped by the strength of where I come from, or by the steady love that's always awaited me there.

To my son, Breck: You are, and will always be, the brightest thing I've ever made. Thank you for your patience, curiosity, and quiet understanding during the long days (and stranger nights) when I slipped into another world to follow this story. Your presence reminds me of why it matters to return. You ground me, even when the writing tries to pull me somewhere else entirely.

To Matt, my husband: Thank you for your patience when the hours got long and the edges of the real world started to blur. For holding steady even when I didn't, and for making room for all of this to exist.

To the friends and loved ones who listened when I needed to speak, who made room for silence when I couldn't find the words, and who showed up without needing explanations— you know who you are. Your presence, your patience, your faith in me… mattered more than I can say.

To the versions of myself that didn't make it here, and to the past that tried—so many times—to convince me I didn't have the right to write any of this: Thank you. You taught me how to reclaim a voice I was never meant to lose.

And finally, to you—yes, you, the reader. Whether you found this book accidentally or followed it here with intention, thank you for stepping inside. For staying. For letting it live in your hands, mind, and maybe even your chest for a little while. Stories like this carry risk, and you made the risk worth it.

There is more to come.

But for now, thank you for everything.

With love and deep gratitude,

—Ophelia Fey

Prologue

Some words were never meant to be spoken.

They are older than language, older than breath—carved not into stone or scripture, but into the marrow of the world itself. You won't find them in books or whispered by candlelight in the mouths of old storytellers. They don't survive in rhyme or riddle. They survive in silence. In the forgotten corners of memory, in the lull between dream and waking. In the stillness after something is lost and just before it's found again.

These words are buried deep—hidden in our sleep, covered by shadow, under the thrum of blood passed down through generations that have long stopped asking what their lineage was meant to protect. And they wait. Not with urgency, but with patience. With purpose.

No one agrees on their origin. Some say they began as prayers—desperate invocations carved into the dark by those who had nothing left but hope. Others believe they were curses, bartered in grief, sharp enough to cut through the veil and fool the heavens into listening. Perhaps they were both. Or neither. Perhaps they simply are—like hunger, or gravity, or the sea.

The first person who spoke them did so without knowing. The glass shimmered, not with light but with attention, and what was once sealed began to stir. It did not open then. Not fully. The path was revealed, but not its destination, and certainly not its cost. And that has always been the danger of mirrors: they show us what's there, but never what waits behind it.

Each time the words are spoken, the door opens a little more. Never wide enough for the world to notice. Just enough for the Hollow to breathe.

Not all who speak the words suffer. Some forget. Some vanish. Some walk away believing it was only a dream.

But the Hollow does not forget.

It listens.

It waits.

And when the right voice speaks again—when the cadence of blood, breath, and name aligns—it will stir.

It will remember the face.

It will remember the wound.

And it will answer.

Introduction

Eira Vardalok hadn't known her real name for years. She was just another name in the system, a number on a chart. Quiet and watchful, her silence unsettled even the most patient foster parents; she moved through the system unnoticed.

Her memories of the past were fragmented: a glass hallway, a woman humming in an unfamiliar language, and a voice whispering her name from behind a closed door. But no one believed her—not the caseworkers, the doctors, or the families who passed her from one home to the next.

So Eira learned to blend in, to survive by staying silent and unnoticed. She pretended to be ordinary.

Until she arrived at Glencrest Academy.

Until she saw the mirror.

Some stories are shaped by fate. Others begin with a choice.

Hers began with a word she didn't recognize but somehow always knew.

I

Part One: What Came Through

She grew up with gaps, not answers. Faces faded,
homes turned cold, and questions went unspoken.
Reports called her quiet, detached, and uncooperative.
But they were wrong.
She noticed everything—shifting buildings, the hum
of metal before disaster.
They thought she was broken. They didn't know she
was already remade.

Chapter One: The Corridor

Eira Vardalok avoided her reflection, especially when she was alone, especially at night, and especially when the silence in a room began to feel like it was listening. When Eira was eight years old, a social worker had pulled her from a smoke-scarred apartment in the dead of winter. The woman, with her clinical smile and coat that smelled like cheap dryer sheets, told Eira she was being given a "fresh start," a new life, a clean slate—as if childhood could be scrubbed like a chalkboard. No one ever asked about what came before, and Eira quickly learned not to bring it up.

By sixteen, she had mastered the unspoken rules of foster care, and none were more important than this one: Don't get noticed. Don't ask questions. Don't stand out. Because the moment you drew attention, good or bad, something was always taken away.

Tonight, Glencrest Academy was cloaked in the kind of silence that didn't feel restful but rather coiled, as though the air itself were holding its breath. The hallway stretched ahead, dim and hollow. The only sounds were the soft, irregular hums from the flickering overhead fluorescents and the distant ticking of radiators that never warmed evenly. The building reeked of damp stone and the mildew of old paper—ancient tomes and forgotten yearbooks sealed away in corners of the school no one visited unless they had to. It was haunted, though not in the way students meant when they giggled about dead nuns or former headmasters. Glencrest didn't need ghosts. It had weight. Memory. It felt like it remembered everything.

Eira sat cross-legged on the cold linoleum floor, her back to a row of unused lockers at the far end of the east wing—an area teachers rarely walked and cameras didn't quite reach. The light above her flickered in slow, uneven pulses, casting brief moments of stillness followed by jerking, unsettling shadows. She didn't mind the flickering. It kept the dark from settling completely, which somehow felt safer.

Then the air changed.

At first, it was subtle, a shift in pressure, like the kind that comes before a thunderstorm. Then, without warning, a breeze stirred through her hair, gentle but unmistakably wrong—because the windows were sealed, the doors locked, and nothing should have moved.

A cold breath licked the nape of her neck, and she flinched instinctively, her entire body going rigid.

Something scraped across the tile floor at the end of the hall—not footsteps, not the familiar thud of shoes or boots, but something slower, like heavy cloth being dragged inch by inch. The sound came with an unnatural rhythm, as if whatever made it didn't quite understand how movement worked.

Then came the light.

It shimmered faintly at the far end of the corridor, not quite white or silver—pale and milky, like moonlight seen through thick fog. It pulsed once, like something breathing.

She stood, barely realizing she was doing it.

"Hello?" she called out, her voice quieter than intended. It sounded swallowed.

No answer came. The light remained still.

But she moved toward it anyway.

Each step felt reluctant, like the floor had grown thicker, heavier, resisting her weight. The hallway seemed to stretch, subtly at first, then more noticeably. Familiar doorways disappeared behind her. Lockers blurred at the edges. The hum of the lights changed pitch.

The world felt… rearranged.

As she neared the light, it split.

A figure appeared inside it.

It stood tall and impossibly still, clothed in a robe of shifting white that shimmered without breeze or breath. Where a face should have been, there was only darkness—an orb of blackness that devoured light rather than reflected it. Yet somehow, it had eyes—deep, bottomless eyes, black as oil and alive in a way that made her bones ache.

Eira stopped walking.

The air thickened with invisible weight, pressing down on her chest, making it hard to breathe. Her thoughts slowed. Her skin crawled, like tiny insects danced just beneath the surface.

Then it spoke.

Not with a mouth, and not in any voice she could place. The sound was felt, not heard—like vibrations inside her teeth, ribcage, and spine. A single word, broken into three pieces, slid into her like ice.

"Sa-lith-a-nor."

She repeated it before she realized she was speaking. The syllables cracked from her lips like a language she wasn't supposed to know, but had always carried in her blood.

As the final syllable left her mouth, the light shattered.

It didn't explode. It fractured—slowly, like glass under pressure—and from those fractures bloomed a mirror.

No frame. No depth. Just a silver surface spreading outward across the wall like a ripple in water.

In it, she saw herself.

But something was wrong.

The girl within it wore her face, but it didn't sit right. Her eyes were too wide, the irises too dark, absorbing light instead of catching it. Her mouth curled into a smile that suggested knowing, knowing, and enjoying something Eira didn't understand. And she didn't blink.

Eira took a single step back.

It moved with Eira as she slowly backed away.

The surface rippled as if alive, like skin stretched over water. For a moment, the girl in the mirror leaned closer, and Eira could swear the glass exhaled.

Then—nothing.

The figure vanished.

Eira tried to run.

Her body didn't listen.

Her limbs froze, muscles tight and trembling. The glass beckoned without words, humming in silence. Her heart pounded hard enough to make her ears ring.

Then something cold and wet pressed against her palm.

She looked down.

It was her hand, but something mirrored it, touching her from the other side.

The mirror began to pull.

Darkness bloomed across her vision, and just before the world gave out—

She woke, lying on the cold floor, gasping for air.

The corridor was empty, the mirror was gone, and the light above her buzzed feebly, as if nothing had happened.

But the air still held that charge, that faint hum of something *alive*.

Eira stood, unsteady. Her legs felt like they remembered being somewhere she had not walked. She turned back toward the wall—but there was only chipped paint and the faint smell of stone dust.

Still, the unease followed her like a second skin.

She moved quickly through the corridor. But every step made the world feel more…off. The overhead lights now flickered in time with her heartbeat. Her shadow lagged behind her, just slightly—half a second late, as though reluctant to follow.

Then came the bell.

Not Glencrest's dull electric chime, but a real bell. Brass, deep-toned. It rang once, slow and resonant, like something from a forgotten church buried beneath centuries.

She passed the stairwell and told herself not to glance sideways..

She failed.

Her reflection stared back, but didn't match her movement. Its head cocked to one side, too far, too slow—like a puppet moved by unseen strings—its lips parting in eerie silence.

She didn't need to hear it to know her fate was beginning.

Salith'anor.

She bolted up the stairs and didn't stop running until she reached her dorm.

Her hands shook as she turned the lock, then backed away from the mirror above the sink. For now, it showed only her—pale, breathing too fast, but real.

She dropped her bag, pulled up her sleeve, and stared at the mark on her wrist.

It looked like a brand, but there had been no flame—only the word—only the glass. And this symbol—curved and sharp, like a spiral, like an eye—was now etched into her skin —something that saw her before she knew it existed.

With numb fingers, she grabbed a pen and sketched the shape in her notebook. She'd seen sigils before—she had an entire bookmarked folder of occult research—but nothing she found matched this.

It wasn't Norse. Not Greek. Not even Enochian.

But it was something. And it was part of her now.

Her phone buzzed.

A message from an unknown number: **"You spoke it."**

Her stomach dropped.

Another buzz. A second message: **"It heard you."**

Her hands trembled as she picked the phone up again, but the messages had vanished.

Only two empty speech bubbles remained.

Then her lamp flicked on—without touch, without warning.

The mirror above the sink began to fog, though the air remained cold. Letters etched themselves into the glass, stroke by stroke.

"Welcome."

The mark on her wrist glowed faintly, pulsing in sync with her racing pulse.

The light went out again.

Darkness.

But not silence.

A whisper—so close it felt like breath on her cheek—unfurled from the room's corners.

"Eira..."

She didn't scream.

She picked up the notebook again and, beneath the symbol, wrote the word: *Salith'anor.*

Then she whispered to the dark, "What are you?"

No answer came—only a soft *thud.*

From the closet.

She turned slowly, and her hand moved without consent. The air felt full, thick, and almost wet, like breath from something too large to see.

She opened the closet door.

Empty.

Except for a pane of glass that hadn't been there before.

It was oval. Antique. Hung on the back wall like it belonged.

And in its depths—something worse than a reflection.

A hallway of ancient stone. Lit by flame. And at its center, a child.

The child looked up. Mouth open.

A shrieking sound surrounded her, and then it screamed.

Salith'anor!

The light flared again. Then—blackness.

When she looked again, the closet was empty.

But the symbol on her wrist still pulsed.

And the mirror was still somewhere.

Prepared.

* * *

She stood in the center of her room, wrapped in the low buzz of electric quiet, the kind of silence that doesn't comfort but stretches itself too thin, like it's listening from the corners, waiting for her to let her guard down. Her arms were crossed tight against her chest, not because she was cold, though she was, but because her body didn't know what else to do with itself anymore. It felt like a shell someone else had climbed into.

Everything familiar had taken on a slight distortion: the photos tacked to the wall no longer looked like memories but evidence; the books on her shelf seemed rearranged, not by hand but by intention; even the air smelled different, touched with a metallic tang, like rust stirred into breath.

She tried to convince herself this was trauma manifesting in paranoia, that the human brain was more than capable of inventing entire nightmares in the absence of sleep, comfort, or continuity—but that idea dissolved the moment her eyes fell again on the symbol burning beneath her skin.

It had no origin, at least not one she could find in the twenty-seven search tabs she'd opened on her battered laptop, none of which gave her anything resembling truth—just pages that glitched when she typed the word, or redirected to empty domains, or worse, to obscure forums filled with people asking the same question she hadn't dared to say aloud: *Has anyone else seen it?*

She turned the computer off. Its screen stayed black a moment too long, as if reluctant to let her go.

In the mirror, her reflection remained obedient. It blinked when she blinked. It moved when she moved. But there was something wrong in the timing—barely a fraction of a second delay, subtle enough to dismiss if she hadn't already seen what a *true* mismatch looked like. Now, even perfect mimicry seemed suspect.

When she finally lay down, the bed felt unfamiliar under her weight, as if the mattress remembered someone else. Sleep did not come gently. When it arrived, it came like a hand over her face.

She found herself walking again, barefoot on ancient stone slick with damp, the walls pressed in tight, breathing behind them like lungs buried in mortar. The mirrors stretched on either side of her—tall, thin, warped things that reflected more than her body. They reflected possibilities, refusals, and pieces of her she didn't remember becoming.

And then the voices began—not whispered, not screamed, just spoken in that same slow, deliberate tone, as if the words themselves had teeth. Every reflection opened its mouth at once.

"Salith'anor."

One stepped forward—her, and not her. Pale. Hollow-eyed. Her mouth moved again, slower this time, as if savoring the syllables.

"We have been waiting."

She woke with a start, drenched in sweat, the bedsheets twisted like restraints around her limbs. Her breath came sharp and dry, like she'd been drowning far away. A sharp knock rattled her door once, then nothing.

She didn't answer.

Didn't dare.

She moved to the door on legs that barely listened and peered through the peephole, expecting to see nothing but shadow.

There was no one there.

But something had been left on the floor just outside.

Small. Oval. Facedown.

Its back was etched in a swirling spiral that almost perfectly matched the shape that now lived in her skin. She stared at it through the crack in the door, heart pounding, jaw locked, her entire body screaming not to open it.

But something inside her—quieter, older—was already reaching for the handle.

She didn't touch it.

Not yet.

Instead, she backed away slowly, eyes never leaving the mirror's outline. The lights above her buzzed, flickered, then dimmed. And in the reflection of the window across the room, she saw it clearly:

Her shadow had moved.

But she hadn't.

Chapter Two: The Mark

Eira didn't sleep anymore that night. Her body hovered in that strange space between wakefulness and dreams, where thoughts blurred into fragmented images. Every time she closed her eyes, the same visions returned: the glass in the closet, the stone hallway, and the child whispering the word that now felt etched into her skin.

Salith'anor.

It repeated in her mind like a melody, low and haunting, a voice she couldn't place but somehow knew.

When morning light finally seeped through the blinds, Eira sat up without hesitation. The air in her dorm room felt heavy, as if it had settled into something unfamiliar. The usual creaks of the floorboards and the hum of the pipes were muffled, distant. The space no longer felt like hers.

She pulled on her jacket, covering the mark on her wrist. It pulsed faintly, like a second heartbeat. The closet door stood ajar, and the reflective surface inside caught the pale morning light. Her likeness stared back, passive and unremarkable, yet something in her gaze felt off—a subtle tilt of the head, a dullness inside her eyes.

Eira didn't linger. She turned away and left the room.

The school hallways buzzed with the rhythm of a weekday morning. Locker doors slammed, and voices overlapped in a blur of conversations. It all felt muted to Eira, as if she were observing it from behind a pane of glass.

She kept her head down, clutching her books tightly. Then she felt a presence—a pressure, like a stare pressing against her back.

She glanced up.

At the end of the hallway stood a person she didn't recognize. This being had posture that was too still, the gaze too direct. It didn't look away when her eyes met his. Instead, the expression sharpened with an unwavering stare.

Then it turned the corner and vanished.

Eira's breath caught in her throat. She scanned the hallway, but no one else seemed to notice. She forced herself to keep moving, her wrist stinging beneath her sleeve.

Ms. Harlan paced the room in literature class, reciting Poe with theatrical flair. Eira heard none of it. Her thoughts kept returning to the creature she just saw. The stare hadn't been curious—it had been knowing.

When the bell rang, she lingered, letting the room empty. As she stepped into the hallway, a voice called her name.

"Eira."

She turned. A boy stood there, watching her.

He approached slowly, his steps deliberate.

"You said it," he said.

"Said what?" she asked, her voice steady despite the unease coiling in her chest.

"The word. Salith'anor."

Her heart dropped.

"Who are you?" she demanded.

"Zak," he replied. "And I've been waiting for someone else to say it."

Eira crossed her arms. "You need to tell me what's going on."

"You probably don't remember me in the lecture hall," Zak said quietly.

"You were in that class?"

"I was in there for a reason."

"You followed me?"

"No." He hesitated. "I waited. There's a difference."

He glanced down the hall, his expression unreadable. "I don't know everything. But I know enough. Once you speak it, it knows you. And it doesn't let go."

Eira pulled back her sleeve, revealing the mark.

Zak's eyes didn't widen, didn't flinch. "Yeah," he said softly. "Mine fades away at times."

That evening, they met in the old library—a forgotten corner of the campus where time seemed to move more slowly. The heavy oak doors creaked as they opened, and the air inside was thick with the scent of aged paper and polished wood. Tall, narrow windows let in soft light, illuminating motes of dust that hung suspended in the air.

The library was silent, its stillness weighted, as if the walls held memories of every student who had passed through. Zak led her to a secluded alcove tucked between shelves of mythology and ancient languages. A single reading lamp cast a warm glow over the table, a small island of light in the shadows.

Zak set down a leather-bound notebook, scuffed at the edges. Its pages were filled with messy ink lines, sketches of strange symbols, and fragmented notes. Eira flipped through it slowly. On the third page, she froze.

The symbol from her wrist stared back at her, nearly identical.

"You've seen others?" she asked.

Zak nodded. "Only twice. One didn't last long. The other..." He hesitated. "I don't know what happened to her. But the school keeps records. Shadow files, they're called. Once someone's marked, they're... different."

"Different how?"

"They stop being themselves."

Eira fell silent, setting the notebook down.

"I feel like I'm dreaming," she admitted. "But it's not my dream. It's like I'm trapped in someone else's memory."

"That's how it starts," Zak said. "It slips inside. You won't always know what's yours anymore."

A draft passed through the alcove, and one of the lights

flickered.

"There's more," Zak continued. "These marks aren't random. They appear on certain people—people connected to the old blood."

"What old blood?"

Zak hesitated. "I think it's ancestral. Families tied to the original tongues. Languages older than Latin. Older than runes."

Eira touched her wrist, the mark itching inside her skin.

"What does the word mean?" she asked. "Salith'anor?"

Zak's expression grew tired. "I've only found one translation. It's not exact, but it's close."

"Tell me."

"It means 'The voice before the voice.'"

Later, back in her room, Eira sat on the floor in the dark. Her back pressed against the foot of the bed, her eyes fixed on the closet door. The glass inside remained still, but she couldn't shake the feeling that it was watching her.

She stood and walked to the closet, pushing the door open. A chill brushed her skin, though there were no vents nearby. She stepped closer, the floor creaking below her.

The reflection showed her room perfectly—the bed, the nightstand, the lamp—but her likeness lagged, a fraction of a second behind. She raised her hand slowly. The girl in the image followed, her movements slightly off, as if reality were struggling to keep up.

Then the background shifted.

Her room's reflection faded, replaced by stone walls etched with symbols. Torches flickered to life, casting shadows that danced along a dim corridor.

And then she saw herself.
Not her reflection—another her.

This version of her stood stiffly, her posture unnatural. Her eyes were completely black, void of light.

The other Eira didn't mimic her movements. She moved independently, stepping closer until only inches separated them.

The surface rippled.

Eira gasped and stepped back, but her legs wouldn't move. Her knees locked, her feet rooted to the floor.

The glass-Eira pressed a hand against the panel. On the other side, it bowed outward, like liquid metal.

And then it smiled.
Not kindly. Not with warmth. It was a smile that didn't belong on her face.

Eira's breath hitched.

The whispers came next—layered voices, ancient and dry,

repeating the same word over and over.

"Return. Return. Return."

The surface vibrated, the torches in the vision flaring wildly.

The twin mouthed one final word.

"Soon."

Eira stumbled backward, her heart racing. The corridor dissolved back into the reflection of her room.

Her face returned, but something about it still felt wrong.

She grabbed her notebook, her fingers trembling. When she turned to the page with the symbol, her heart sank. The ink had spread, and the mark was darker and more defined.

A new line of text had appeared, written in a language she didn't know but somehow understood:

"The gate opens with you."

In the reflection, her image remained still.

Her eyes, darker than before, locked onto Eira's. Expecting.

***

The next morning, Eira avoided looking at herself entirely. She dressed quickly, keeping her back to the closet, and left her room without glancing inside. The weight of the mark on her wrist felt heavier, as if it were pulling her toward something she couldn't see.

The hallways were quieter than usual, the air thick with an unspoken tension. Eira kept her head down, avoiding eye contact. She didn't want to see the boy again or hear what he might say next.

But as she rounded the corner, there he was.

Zak stood by her locker, his back against the wall, his hands tucked into his pockets. He didn't smile or speak, just watched her approach.

"What do you want?" she asked, her voice sharper than she intended.

"You saw it, didn't you?" he asked. "In the glass."

Eira didn't answer. She didn't need to.

"It's happening faster for you," he said. "That's not a good sign."

"What do you mean?"

Zak pushed himself off the wall. "The reflections. The whispering. They're getting stronger."

"How do you know?"

"Because I've seen it before," he said. "With the others."

Eira's grip on her books tightened. "What really happened to them, Zak?"

He looked away. "They're gone, Eira."

The day passed in a blur. Eira moved through her classes like a ghost, her thoughts consumed by the mark on her wrist and the boy's words. She couldn't focus or shake the feeling that something was closing in around her.

When the final bell rang, she didn't go back to her dorm. Instead, she found herself walking to the old library. She didn't know why, but she needed answers, and Zak seemed to be the only one with them.

The library was empty, and the air was colder than before. Eira made her way to the alcove where they had met the night before. Zak was already there, his notebook open on the table.

"You came back," he said, his voice neutral.

"I need to know more," she said.

Zak hesitated, then nodded. "There's a story. An old one. About a language that predates everything we know. They say it was spoken by the first of us, before time was even measured."

"What does that have to do with me?"

"The marks," he said. "They're part of it. A connection to that language. And the glass… it's a gate."

Eira's heart skipped a beat. "A gate to what?"

Zak didn't answer right away. "I don't know," he admitted finally. "But I think they're tied to the archaic blood. To the families who carried the language."

Eira's mind raced. "How do we stop it?"

Zak closed his notebook. "We don't," he said quietly. "We can't. Once it starts, it doesn't stop."

Eira stared at him, her chest tight. "That's it? That's all you know?"

"It's all I've been able to find," he said. "But there's something else. The glass… it doesn't just show you. It listens."

Eira's breath caught. "What do you mean?"

"It responds to the word. To Salith'anor. That's why it's important. It's like a key."

Eira's wrist burned, the mark throbbing in time with her pulse. "What happens when it opens?"

Zak met her gaze. "I don't know," he said. "But I think we're about to find out."

* * *

That night, Eira couldn't stay in her room. The air felt too heavy, the walls too close. She left the dorm and walked, her steps aimless, her mind racing.

She found herself in front of the library again. The heavy doors creaked as she pushed them open, echoing through the empty halls. She didn't know what she was looking for, but she couldn't shake the feeling that she needed to be there.

The alcove was dark, the reading lamp extinguished. Zak wasn't there. Eira hesitated, then sat down at the table, her fingers tracing the leather cover of his notebook.

She opened it, flipping through the pages until she found her symbol again. The lines seemed to shift underneath her gaze, twisting and turning into something new.

A voice muttered behind her.

"It's too late."

Eira spun around. Zak stood in the shadows, his face pale, his eyes empty.

"What do you mean?" she asked, her voice barely above a whisper.

"The gate," he said. "It's opening."

Eira's heart pounded. "What do we do?"

Zak moved closer, his voice low. "We can't stop it. But I think we can slow it down."

"How?"

"The portal needs the word. It needs Salith'anor. If we don't speak it, we can buy time."

Eira's mind raced. "And then what?"

Zak didn't answer. He didn't need to.

The air around them shifted, growing colder. The lights flickered, and a low drone filled the room.

Zak's eyes widened. "It's happening."

Eira turned toward the nearest panel of glass. The surface rippled, the images distorting.

The whispers grew louder, more insistent.

"Return. Return. Return."

Zak grabbed her hand. "Don't speak it. No matter what."

Eira nodded, her throat tight. Her mouth trying to voice the word against her will.

The panel bulged, like something was trying to push through. The whispers turned into a roar, the air vibrating with their intensity.

And then, silence.

The surface darkened. The voices stopped.

Eira's wrist burned, the mark glowing faintly under her sleeve.

Zak's grip on her hand tightened. "It's not over," he said. "It's never over."

Eira didn't respond. She didn't need to.
   The gate had opened.
   And it was awaiting them.

Chapter Three: Where the Stones Still Speak

The mark had changed overnight.

Eira woke to a pulsing warmth on her wrist, the triskelion now sharper, darker, more defined—as if etched into her skin with fire rather than memory. Though it hadn't moved, she swore it was alive. She could feel the outline of it on the surface, like breath trapped in her frame.

By midday, she was back in the shadows of Glencrest. Her world blurred into a quiet purr—the shifting of books in lockers, the drone of lectures, and the whispering cadence she refused to look into. She met Zak near the abandoned east stairwell, his notebook tucked under one arm and the familiar look of dread behind his pale eyes.

"You've seen it again?," she interrogated.

He didn't answer. Instead, he handed her a page—a sketch of the triskelion, inked in harsh, curved lines. It pulsed slightly, as if her touch gave it breath.

"The gate is waking," he muttered. "And it's not just here."

After hours, Eira followed Zak to the old records room under library that night. Cobwebbed shelves, locked drawers, and dusty binders made it feel more crypt than archive. Zak worked silently, brushing dust off yellowing parchment and sorting through diagrams like someone half-mad.

"This place was built over something older," he said. "Some of the chapel's foundations date back to Norse settlers. I found references to a 'hidden triskelion'—a guardian symbol placed on bloodlines tied to the sea."

He pulled a folder from the bottom drawer and opened it, revealing an aged vellum page sketched with the triskelion, surrounded by spiraling script.

"They used to carve it into rock along the shore," he added. "Mostly in the Channel Islands. Sark. Alderney. Guernsey. But the Isle of Man is the only place where they claim the symbol came from something… living."

Eira stared at the sketch. "Living?"

He nodded. "They said it moved when you weren't looking."

Eira ran her fingers over the vellum, and the room shifted slightly, like the ground beneath them had exhaled.

"Something's changing," she said quietly. "I feel like I'm not all here anymore."

Zak closed the folder and handed it to her. "Then we follow it. This started in the past."

She slept that night with the triskelion still burning her skin. The dream came as it always did—fog, mirrors, and a voice that sounded like her own but older, richer, and more certain.

But this time, when she reached out, her hand passed through.

And the dream did not end.

Fog curled over the black cliffs of an unfamiliar coastline. The sea crashed in rhythms that felt like breathing. The air smelled of salt and pine, and somewhere in the distance, a bell tolled slowly.

The Channel Islands. But not as they were now.

The village was lit with torches, its pathways winding between stone huts and longboats pulled ashore. Women carried woven baskets, men wore hides over armor, and every so often, Eira caught flashes of symbols etched into the doors—runes she had seen before only in dreams.

Two figures stood at the water's edge.

One—a tall, dark-haired woman wrapped in deep blue wool, eyes as sharp as ebony.

The other—a man with streaks of silver through his beard, one hand wrapped around a staff marked with spirals, the other resting gently on the woman's lower back.

"I felt her pass through," the woman said. "This time, she didn't land on the water."

"She's marked," the man replied. "The sea chose her."

They turned toward the hills where a faint glow pulsed behind a ring of standing stones.

"She's not of this world," the woman said.

"Not yet," the man answered. "But she's waking."

And in the reflection of the water, the triskelion spun once before fading into stillness.

The woman turned slowly, her wool cloak catching the wind as she ascended the path toward the standing stones. The man followed, his staff dragging lightly in the Earth, carving a trail beside hers. They passed between the monoliths with reverence, pausing at the largest stone in the center. It was etched with deep grooves worn by weather and time, but the shape of the triskelion was unmistakable, illuminated faintly by the moonlight that broke through the clouds.

"It was here she crossed last," the woman murmured. "Before the last gate sealed."

The man studied the stone with narrowed eyes. "You believe

she's the same soul reborn?"

"No," she said. "I believe she's the same soul continued."

He said nothing, but his fingers tightened around the shaft of his staff.

Under their feet, the ground trembled slightly, like the pulse of something vast awakening far below. The woman knelt and pressed her palm to the soil. Her breath caught.

"She's closer now. This place remembers her."

Down in the village, the air shifted. Flames in the torches flickered unnaturally. Animals stirred in their pens, restless. An elder sitting by the hearth turned her head sharply, as if hearing something only she could understand. Children stopped playing and stared toward the cliffs.

Back among the stones, the woman, Runa, now named, closed her eyes.

"She is afraid, but not running. Curious, but not unguarded."

Varg looked at her, his voice low. "And if she refuses to return?"

Runa stood and brushed her palms against her robe. "Then the mirror will open another way. But it will not be kind."

They descended together, silent under stars. The triskelion at the heart of the stones pulsed once, briefly casting their shadows long behind them.

In her bed in Glencrest, Eira twisted in her sheets, caught in the layers of the dream that now felt more memory than vision. The smell of sea salt still clung to her senses, and the sound of low and rhythmic chanting rattled faintly behind her ears like wind against glass.

She sat up sharply.

The room was silent. Her hand ached with a new depth, and when she turned on the light, she saw it—not the mark itself, but the skin around it.

Bruised.

Marked.

Changed.

She stood and walked to the mirror.

It no longer reflected her room. Instead, it shimmered faintly, like a screen filled with fog.

And for just a second, she saw the woman in blue standing among the stones.

Observing her.

Prepared.

The next morning, Eira's arm burned with a dull ache that refused to fade. She pulled her sleeve lower, avoiding her reflection as she left her dorm. The air in the hallway felt heavier, and the lights flickered more than usual. Her step echoed strangely, as if the ground beneath her feet was slightly out of sync.

She met Zak in the library again, the records room now their unofficial base. He sat at the table, his notebook open and filled with frantic sketches—triskelions, runes, and maps of the Channel Islands overlaid with faint, spidery lines.

"It's getting worse," he said without looking up.

Eira didn't reply. She didn't need to.

"The gateway isn't just waking," he continued. "It's opening. The mirrors merely mark the threshold."

Eira pulled out the folder he'd given her the night before. The parchment sketch of the triskelion seemed darker, the spiraling script around it almost glowing in the dim light.

"What does it mean?" she asked.

Zak finally looked up, his eyes shadowed. "It means we don't have much time."

He pushed a stack of books toward her—old, leather-bound volumes with cracked spines and faded lettering. "These are records from the Channel Islands. Sark, Alderney, Guernsey. They all have stories about the triskelion. But there's one that's different."

He opened a book to a marked page. "The Isle of Man. They say the symbol wasn't just a carving. It was a warning."

Eira's pulse quickened. "A warning of what?"

Zak hesitated. "Of something that was never meant to be found."

The day passed in a haze of research and restless energy. Eira's wrist throbbed in time with her heartbeat, the mark feeling heavier with every passing hour. By evening, the air in the library had grown colder, and the shadows seemed to deepen around them.

Zak's voice broke the quietness. "There's something else."

Eira looked up. "What?"

"The woman in your dreams. Runa."

"What about her?"

Zak's expression was unreadable. "She's real. Or she was."

He pushed another folder across the table. Inside were faded photographs of carvings and ancient etchings on stone. At the center of one was a figure—a woman in a flowing cloak, her posture regal, her eyes staring straight into the camera as if she could see through time.

"They called her the Keeper of the Stones," Zak said. "She was part of a bloodline tied to the triskelion. They say she could walk between worlds."

Eira's hand went to her wrist. "And you think that's who I'm seeing?"

Zak didn't respond. He didn't need to.

That night, Eira didn't sleep. She sat on the floor of her room, the folder open in front of her, the vellum sketch of the triskelion spread across her lap. The air around her felt charged, as if the walls held their breath.

She traced the lines of the triskelion with her finger, her movements slow and deliberate. The symbol seemed to shift beneath her touch, the edges blurring and reforming.

And then she heard a low, rhythmic chanting, faint but unmistakable.

It was the same sound from her dream.

Eira stood, her heart racing. The air in the room felt thicker now, the shadows deeper. She walked to the mirror, her image wavering in the glass.

For a moment, nothing happened.

And then the haze appeared.

It curled and twisted, filling the surface until it cleared, revealing the standing stones. Runa stood among them, her cloak whipping in the wind, her eyes fixed on Eira.

"You are closer," Runa said, her voice a whisper carried on the air.

Eira didn't move. "Closer to what?"

Runa trod forward, her hand reaching to touch the mirror's surface. "To understand."

The ground below Eira's feet trembled, a faint vibration that grew stronger with each passing second. The walls of her room seemed to shift, the edges blurring like the visions in the glass.

"What is happening?" Eira asked, her voice barely steady.

Runa's gaze didn't waver. "The gate is opening. And you are the key."

The room shook harder, books falling from shelves, the floor buckling her. Eira stumbled, her hand reaching out to steady herself.

And then, as quickly as it began, it stopped.

The room stilled. The mirror cleared.

Eira stood frozen, her wrist still throbbing, the mark pulsating like a heartbeat.

She turned back...

Runa was gone.

But the triskelion remained, etched into the glass, spinning slowly.

Ready and waiting.

* * *

The next day, Eira avoided Zak. She couldn't face him, not yet. The weight of what she had seen—what she had felt—was too much. The mark on her burned constantly now, a constant reminder of something she didn't understand but couldn't ignore.

She moved through the day in a daze; her steps were mechanical, and her mind was elsewhere. The air around her felt different, charged with something she couldn't name. Every time she passed a mirror, she caught herself looking for the fog, for Runa, for the triskelion.

But there was nothing.

Until there was.

It happened during lunch, in the crowded cafeteria. Eira was sitting alone, her food untouched, her mind spinning with thoughts of standing stones and ancient bloodlines.

And then she saw it.

She saw Runa in the reflection of the glass window across the room. She stood among the students, her cloak replaced by modern clothes, her dark hair pulled back, and her eyes as sharp as ever.

She was watching Eira.

Eira froze, her heart pounding.

Runa's lips moved, forming words Eira couldn't hear.

And then she was gone.

Eira stood abruptly, her chair scraping against the floor. She didn't care about the stares, the whispers.

She had to find Zak.

She found him in the library, poring over another stack of books. He looked up as she approached, his expression guarded.

"I saw her," Eira said, her voice shaking. "Runa. She was here."

Zak's eyes widened slightly. "Here? At Glencrest?"

Eira nodded. "In the cafeteria. In the reflection of the window."

Zak closed his book slowly. "Then it's happening faster than I thought."

He stood, grabbing his notebook. "We need to go back to the records room. Now."

They moved quickly, their steps echoing through the empty halls. The air grew colder as they descended the stairs, the lights flickering overhead.

The records room was waiting, its shelves filled with secrets Eira wasn't sure she was ready to uncover.

But it was too late to turn back now.

The gate was opening.

And she was the key.

Chapter Four: Three Legs, One Gate

The image of the woman in blue lingered in Eira's mind long after the mirror dimmed, like a shadow that had carved itself into the walls of her thoughts. There was something in the way the woman stood—unnaturally still, like a figure in a painting, waiting for the moment when no one was watching to move again. Morning light filtered through the dorm blinds, pale and cold, yet her room felt heavier, as if something unseen had lingered through the night, its presence still pressing against the edges of the space.

She dressed slowly, her movements deliberate, her wrist aching under sleeve of her jacket. The mark had changed again. What had once been a faint, intricate design was now darker, sharper, as though the lines were trying to push through her skin. She couldn't stop rubbing her thumb over it, feeling the raised edges, the heat that seemed to radiate from down under.

She kept seeing the woman in her mind—standing among the stones, wrapped in blue, her dark eyes fixed on something Eira couldn't see.

Her presence lingered, heavy and unyielding.

In the library, Eira found a corner that swallowed sound. The stacks of forgotten books loomed around her, their spines thick with dust, the air still and heavy. She pulled her journal from her bag and flipped to the page where she'd sketched the symbol. It had changed again. What had once been crisp and deliberate now blurred at the edges, as though it had shifted when she wasn't looking. Residing were faint lines of writing curved and branched from the page, written in a language she didn't recognize but somehow understood.

Zak arrived twenty minutes late, his eyes dark and tired, his shoulders hunched as though he carried something unseen.

"You okay?" she asked.

He didn't answer, only stared at the page she held open.

"You saw her," he said.

Eira nodded. "Through the mirror. I think she saw me, too."

Zak sank into the chair opposite her and pulled a worn book from his coat. "I brought this. It's from an estate collection. Hidden in a false back inside an old Bible. I was trying to trace the mark."

She flipped through the pages. The paper was thin, the ink uneven and hand-drawn. Symbols repeated in strange sequences—diagrams of doorways, fractured copies, and altars. Some of the faces were scratched out, as though someone had tried to erase them entirely.

One image stopped her. It was the triskelion, but not flat. Carved into a stone doorway, twisted slightly in perspective, with mirrored shards lining the entry.

"This one," she said softly.

"That's the one they tried to bury," Zak said. "The one under Glencrest."

She looked up. "It's here?" Eira blinked. "How do you know?"

Zak flipped a few pages forward. "There's a reference here. Latin, barely legible—speculum clauditur sub sacro lapide— 'the reflection is sealed by the sacred stone.' And the dates match the oldest records of the chapel's foundation. They built over it. On purpose."

"Below the chapel. Behind a false wall. I think we can get to it. But I don't think it wants to stay sealed."

Eira hesitated. "What makes you say that?"

Zak rolled up his sleeve. His arm bore a faint mark now, different from hers but shaped from the same language.

"It showed up again three nights ago. After I dreamt about water coming through the cracks."

They stared at each other.

"Then let's go," she said.

The chapel was empty. Old stone echoed under their steps as they moved past the altar, candles long burned out, the air stale with dust. Zak led her to a side wall where ancient wood met stone. He pressed his hand along a seam, and with a faint click, a section shifted inward.

Behind it: stairs.

They descended slowly. Eira kept one hand on the cold wall, the other instinctively over her wrist. As they moved lower, a low resonance filled the space—not quite a sound, but not silence, like standing near a humming wire.

The stairs ended in a room carved from the cliff itself. Damp, rough-hewn, and half-collapsed. But at the center, untouched by time, stood a mirror taller than either of them. Its frame was metal, etched with hundreds of the same triskelion pattern. Its surface, however, did not reflect.

It moved.

Soft, like a film of water constantly rolling.

Zak approached it carefully.

"It doesn't show anything from this side," he said.

Eira stepped beside him.

The air shifted. The mirror rippled. And then, faint and slow, a reflection formed.

Not one of them.

But somewhere else. Stone. Blue. Firelight. And a single standing figure with dark eyes and a cloak made of woven hair.

Eira stepped back. "That's her."

Zak didn't move.

"What does she want?" Eira faintly said.

He answered quietly. "Not what. Who."

* * *

The glass shimmered again. Her mark burned hot, and the bruising around it cracked slightly. She watched as something in her skin shifted.

"This isn't just a symbol," she breathed. "It's a key."

Zak nodded. "And a lock. At the same time."

They stood in stillness. The mirror began to glow faintly, casting pale silver light over the chamber. Symbols around the frame brightened in sequence. And then the humming deepened.

It became a vibration inside their chests.

A tall, faceless shape moved behind the woman in blue. Its hands were wrong—too many fingers, too long, jointed in places no hand should be. The movement was fluid, almost boneless, like limbs suspended in deep water, swaying with a current no one could see. The air around Eira chilled as if the shape exhaled frost, and she felt the hair on her arms rise in response.

Eira turned. "We shouldn't be here."

Zak agreed, but his eyes didn't leave what he was witnessing

Then the woman lifted her hand and pressed her palm to the other side of the glass. Eira's wrist seared in response. The pain nearly dropped her.

And in her mind, a voice. Not spoken and not imagined.

"She crossed once. She can do it again."

Eira clutched Zak's arm. "We need to close it."

He reached for the frame, his fingers tracing the ancient metal. The patterns flickered and pulsed like a heartbeat, and the mirror pulsed in turn.

She turned back. Her reflection had returned.

But she wasn't alone.

In the space behind her face, another hovered—not visible, just felt. A presence that breathed her breath and blinked just a second behind her.

"It knows I see it!" she exclaimed.

Zak finally pulled her back.

They didn't run. They didn't speak until they were back under the gray sky outside the chapel.

Eira looked down at her wrist. The skin had sealed again, but the glow hadn't faded. Something turned.

They walked in quiet through the campus paths, taking the long way back to the dorms. Eira's thoughts moved more slowly now, heavy like fog. The further they got from the chapel, the more it all felt like something she might have imagined. Almost.

Zak broke the silence. "I don't think she's a guardian."

Eira glanced over. "You mean the woman in blue?"

He nodded. "She didn't try to stop you from seeing. Or hearing. She invited you."

Eira shook her head. "Then what is she?"

He took a long breath. "A guide, maybe. Or a bridge.

Between this side and whatever's behind the it."

She slowed. "Why you too, Zak? You weren't there. I never brought you into it."

He looked at her, something unreadable in his expression. "When I was a kid, I nearly drowned off the coast of Sark. My parents were visiting family. I was seven. They found me unconscious, face down, near the tide pools. But I remember everything. The stone arch just below the surface. The sound. Not waves—something else. A voice that wasn't spoken aloud. I've been hearing it again. After my parents passing…Well, That's why I came to Glencrest. But I also think I needed to find you."

Eira stopped, looking at him with gloom. "You think it's the same thing."

"I know it is. I've seen her before. Not her face, but the blue. The stone. The water. I didn't remember until I saw you sketching the mark."

They reached the edge of the commons, and the crowd returned—students streaming from classes, heads bent to phones, backpacks bouncing. Life, utterly untouched by what waited directly under their feet of the chapel floor.

Back in her dorm, Eira sat at the foot of her bed for a long time. She didn't move or reach for her notebook or journal. Instead, she stared at the closed closet door, where the mirror sat quietly behind it.

She stood. Opened the door. Pulled the mirror forward.

The surface was still.

But her reflection was not—its head tilted just slightly, a sliver of a grin already forming before her lips had moved. The pupils were too wide for the morning light, and the way it held her gaze felt less like mimicry and more like study.

It smiled before she did.

A small thing, not enough to scream about, but enough to freeze her feet: her eyes remained locked on it, unable to blink, as if blinking might let it slip further through. Her lips were still, but in the glass, they curved.

She backed away.

The mirror didn't return to normal.

It stayed that way for minutes—her face distorted by fractions. Subtle shifts in breath, in posture, in how its eyes tracked hers a moment too late.

And then it stopped. The image of herself aligned. Her breath synced. Her face, her own.

Except she no longer felt alone in her head.

She turned to leave the room.

But the glass shining back at her seemed to blink.

Not her. Not what she saw of herself.

Closing to darkness and relighting in cadence.

Once.

Twice.

Then the glass cracked—just a hairline, splitting across the center of the triskelion symbol that had begun to surface from beneath the silver. A whisper bled through it like vapor, curling into the room.

Not words.

Just breath.

And the sound of footsteps. From inside the glass.

II

Part Two : Who Stayed Behind

*They were here before the names, before the stories,
before the first marks of ink on parchment. The land
never needed to record them; it carried their presence
in stone, salt, and blood that never faded. No temples
were raised for them, no graves dug to hold them.
They lingered in the wind along the cliffs and the
silence that chose its moments to speak. They did not
guard the gate. They remained, long after it had
crumbled.*
This is what they called those Who Stayed Behind.

Chapter Five: The Ones Who Wait Beneath the Tide

Long before the girl ever reached for the mirror—before her name drifted like smoke through the cracked silence of that old place—two figures waited. They lived not in exile, but in quiet defiance, perched on the cragged edge of a cliff where the earth met the sea with a kind of reverent violence. Runa and Varg had built their home there not atop the land, but inside it—woven into the rock and salt like veins beneath skin. The villagers never asked where they came from. They simply knew to leave them be.

The world had turned its face from the old ways, from the blood rituals and whispered truths etched into bone and bark. But the old ways had not forgotten the world. And they had not forgotten those who carried them. The sea still whispered names long buried, and when it spoke Runa's, it did so with reverence.

She had not been born in the way others were, with midwives smiling and parents weeping with joy. Runa arrived beneath a sky split open by a red eclipse, her first cry swallowed by wind that howled like something ancient and displeased. The three midwives who delivered her refused to speak afterward. One left the village entirely. Another took a vow of silence and disappeared into the mountain. The third—her eyes never stopped watering, as if trying to wash away what they'd seen.

Her mother bled out before anyone thought to say the name aloud. And no one, not even the priests, dared finish the prayer that trembled on her lips.

Runa was raised not by tradition but by rhythm—the rhythm of wind against stone, of tide against cliff, of breath drawn in ritual rather than necessity. Moonwater touched her skin before she could stand. Her meals were served in bowls carved with sigils no one dared interpret. She did not ask for bedtime stories. She woke speaking of dreams that did not belong to her.

When she laughed, it sounded wrong. Not evil—just misplaced, like the echo of a chapel hymn in a cellar. She did not move quickly or loudly, but her stillness commanded more attention than any raised voice. Animals followed her at a distance. Children avoided her shadow.

The land responded to her. She knew when storms would break before the clouds turned. She knew where not to step in the fields, where the bones had been buried too shallow. Shapes she traced in soil appeared days later in moss along the cliffs, carved by no hand. She bore no tattoos, no visible sigils, but the earth seemed to know her shape like memory knows grief.

Varg was not from there. Not from anywhere, really. As a boy, he arrived across the sea, washed ashore on the back of a storm with no ship to claim him. The monks who found him said he clung to driftwood carved in a language no one recognized. He spoke no words—not in their tongue nor any other. Not for nine full years. When he finally opened his mouth, it was to whisper a name that made a crow fall dead from the sky.

He did not belong, and so he wandered. Hands too skilled for one so young, carving stories into bark and bone, into shells and stone. Always the same symbols—spirals, antlers, eyes. People left him offerings without knowing why: apples, copper, dried lavender. Women called him beautiful. He called no one back. There was a stillness in him, a sorrow that seemed to stretch backwards.

They met where the land turned brackish and the tide moved backward. They did not smile. They simply nodded, as if resuming a conversation that had been interrupted a century ago. From that moment, they moved in tandem—not lovers, not yet, but inevitable.

Their bond was not loud or dramatic. It hummed just beneath notice, like the tremor before a quake. When their hands brushed for the first time, the sea hissed and withdrew for a full minute. No one saw it happen. But after that night, the shoreline began to change. Kelp washed ashore braided. Shells turned inward. Stones arrived warm, as if carried from deep beneath the earth.

They did not age as others did. Their hair silvered but never dulled. Their joints ached only when the sea grew violent. Their shadows stayed sharp even as the sun faltered. Animals lingered near them without fear. Foxes dozed by their door. Birds sang in scales no other creature could mimic.

Some nights, Runa sang to the tide. Her voice was low, shaped like a question never meant to be answered. Varg never asked what the songs meant. He simply stood in the doorway, arms crossed, listening with the patience of stone. Her words didn't need translation. The sea stilled. That was answer enough.

Villagers left tokens once a year on the boundary line: salt, flax, forged iron. They did not call it worship. They called it insurance. They did not understand what was being kept at bay. Only that it remained so. They called Runa and Varg the Keepers.

No one remembered what they kept.

But the cliff remembered.

And when the mark returned—when the mirror stirred itself back into the world—they felt it first. Not as prophecy. But recognition.

That night, they lay together without speaking. Runa's fingers traced the slope of Varg's ribs—not with lust, but with memory. Outside, the sea pulled too far from shore. The wind paused mid-breath. Something had awakened.

They did not fear it.

They had always known it would come back.

* * *

The air that night tasted of salt and metal, a storm heavy in its belly but not yet born. Runa sat cross-legged beside the hearth, her fingers sifting through a bowl of herbs she had already sorted three times. She wasn't looking at them. Her eyes were fixed on the space just beyond the fire's light, where shadow gathered thickly and refused to move. Varg watched her from his place at the table, one hand wrapped around a cup of water gone cold. Neither spoke. They hadn't needed to. The shift had come.

"It felt like a thread being pulled," she said at last, her voice barely above the fire's crackle.

Varg nodded. He had felt it too—beneath the skin, behind

the ribs, like a remembered name that stirred just out of reach. The mark had returned. Not a warning. Not a threat. A calling. A ripple across the deep.

"She's touched it," Runa continued, though she hadn't meant to say it aloud. Her fingers paused, hovering over dried root and crumbled leaf. "The girl. She's spoken the word."

Varg stood slowly, the movement deliberate, as if the act of rising meant he was leaving something behind. He crossed to the shelf built into the stone wall, where a single object rested beneath folded linen: a shard of obsidian, smooth on one side, jagged on the other. It pulsed faintly with warmth, though it had never seen flame. He hadn't touched it in years.

"She doesn't know what it means," he said, more to the stone than to Runa.

"She doesn't have to," Runa replied. "The mirror does."

Beyond their home, the sea moaned softly. Not the roar of waves breaking, but the low, mournful draw of a tide unsure of its place.

Runa rose then too, brushing dried herb dust from her palms. Her robe fell around her like mist rolling from the high stones. "We should prepare," she said, though neither of them yet knew for what. The old ways had never given timelines—only signs, and those came wrapped in silence.

Varg didn't answer, but moved to the hearth, tossing in a handful of crushed rowan berries. The flame shifted color, from gold to deep green, then settled into an oily blue that crackled without smoke. He knelt beside it, the light casting shadows like bone across his face.

"Will she come here?" he asked finally.

Runa hesitated. "Eventually. Or what remains of her will."

They had seen it before, long ago, in fractured visions and

half-forgotten lore. Those who touched the mirror did not remain untouched in return. The word—*Salith'anor*—was not a key or an invitation. It was a mirror itself. It showed not the other side, but the underside. The part hidden beneath names and skin.

"Do you remember the boy with the white hair?" Runa asked, her voice hollow with the weight of memory.

Varg did. Too well. The boy had spoken the word backward, as a dare, carved it into wood with a blade dulled from bone. He was never found, not entirely. Only his shadow, etched into the cliff wall where he'd stood, mouth still open in silent scream.

"This girl is different," he said, though he wasn't sure he believed it.

"She's marked," Runa replied. "But she isn't born from here. That will either save her—or tear her in half."

Outside, the wind rose. It struck the shutter with three sharp knocks. Runa didn't flinch. She crossed to the window, opened it wide, and let the wind flood the room. It circled once, pulled strands of her hair into its current, then vanished through the smokehole above the fire.

"She's dreaming of us," Runa said, voice far away. "She doesn't know yet, but she is."

Varg joined her by the window, his palm brushing the small of her back. Not possessive. Not tender. Grounding. "Then we'll wait," he said, "the way we always have."

They stood like that for a long time, the fire behind them, the sea beyond them, and the girl—not yet broken, not yet whole—somewhere between.

That night, they did not sleep. They took turns walking the perimeter of their land, listening for sounds only the forgotten would recognize: the knock of a bone against iron, the ripple of language in tree bark, the hush between animal footsteps. Everything spoke if you'd learned to hear it.

Runa paused at the boundary stone carved with three concentric spirals. Her fingers hovered over the cold rock. "It's listening again," she whispered. "The cliff remembers."

And indeed it did. Beneath her feet, the soil hummed faintly. Not like music—but like breath.

Back inside, Varg turned over the mirror shard they kept hidden in their lowest drawer. He had once tried to bury it, but the ground spat it back up at his door three nights later. Since then, it stayed within reach but never in sight.

He stared at it now, its surface reflecting nothing, not even flame. He swore he heard the echo of footsteps—faint and fast, like a girl running down a stone hallway. But when he listened harder, it was gone.

In the far corner, where no wind could touch it, a bowl of water began to tremble.

Runa stepped inside and saw it too. She knelt beside it, staring into the rippling surface. "She's afraid," she murmured.

"Good," Varg said, watching the mirror pulse. "That means she hasn't surrendered yet."

They were not prophets. They had no desire to be. They were not guardians, not in the way stories liked to cast such roles. But they were present. They remembered. They endured.

And when the mirror opened again, they would be ready— not with blades or fire, but with the weight of memory sharpened into silence.

Because some things are not meant to be protected.

They are meant to be witnessed.

Chapter Six: Mother, Remember Me

The shore held its breath. Runa stood where the waves once met the stone, her feet bare on the damp rock. Usually eager to embrace the land, the surf lingered offshore, wary of what hid beneath. Heavy with salt, the air clung to her skin like a warning.

Something had shifted.

The clouds above loomed motionless, their silence more ominous than any storm. Varg's presence settled beside her, his bare feet familiar against the stone. She didn't need to look to know he was there—his weight and warmth were as constant as the tides.

"It's near," he said, his voice barely louder than the whisper of the waves.

Runa exhaled slowly. "Closer than before."

The wind, too, had stilled, as though unwilling to touch whatever stirred in the air.

She turned to him, her expression unreadable. Varg's chest bore the marks of ritual—streaks of soot and salt tracing the lines of old scars. His eyes met hers, not searching for answers but for the silent acknowledgment of what they both felt.

"It was quiet for too long," he said.

Runa nodded, her robe clinging to her form, damp from the

mist. He reached out, his hand brushing her arm. The gesture was deliberate, a memory relived in the space of a moment.

"Do you feel it?" she asked.

"Everywhere."

Her fingers found his jaw, tracing the lines of his face with the reverence of someone who knew every scar, every edge. The kind of gaze that came from knowing a man through countless lives.

They stood like that, unmoving, as though the world had paused around them. There was no hollow. No Eira. No mirror. Only the stillness between them was ancient and unyielding.

The moment held, their lips a breath apart but not touching.

They returned to the cave, its walls shimmering faintly as though remembering other nights—nights when blood mixed with seawater and names were whispered into the dark.

The fire still burned inside, but its flames were subdued, bowing like something had passed too close.

Runa moved to the back of the cave, her fingers trailing the carved stone. Varg followed, his presence a steady anchor. No words were needed; the air itself felt dense with unspoken understanding.

The fire flickered again, turning blue briefly before settling back to orange.

A name echoed through the space, unspoken yet clear: Eira.

Then another, softer still: Zak.

Runa stiffened. Varg's gaze sharpened.

"She's finding her way," Runa said.

"Or it's finding her."

The air grew heavier, layered with tension beyond the physical. Runa stepped forward, her movements deliberate.

Varg watched, his hand grazing the scar on his forearm.

"They see only fragments," she murmured. "Pieces of a truth they can't yet hold."

"The whole would break them," Varg replied.

She traced the triskelion carved into the stone, its grooves worn but familiar. Varg's hand covered hers, their fingers intertwining.

A faint glow rose from the symbol, pulsing faintly.

"She doesn't understand the hunger yet," Runa said.

"She will," Varg said. "They always do."

The fire dimmed again, not from wind but from something unseen. Shadows along the walls stretched and twisted, moving independently of the flames.

Runa turned toward one, her eyes narrowing. "Do you see that?"

Varg nodded. "I see too much."

The shadows lingered, their shapes fluid and unnatural.

* * *

Outside, the ocean began to move in ways it shouldn't. The tide no longer obeyed the moon's pull, churning in slow, deliberate spirals as though waiting for something to surface.

Elsewhere, across fragile threads of space, Eira stood before her mirror. Her reflection wavered, shifting in ways that didn't match her movements.

Zak watched from the corner of the room, his breath fogging the glass even though the air was still.

"They're watching," he said.

Eira didn't blink. "Not just watching. Calling."

Her reflection smiled faintly. But it wasn't her smile.

She turned to Zak, her voice barely a whisper. "Something on the other side knows how to wear us."

Zak's face paled, but he didn't look away.

Runa stepped back from the wall, her hand trembling. She hadn't expected the pull to be this strong. Varg steadied her, his hand on her waist.

"I saw her," she whispered.

"In the mirror?"

"No. In the space between."

She looked up, her voice barely a breath. "She saw me, too."

Their foreheads touched, a silent acknowledgment of the danger they both felt.

"We don't have long," she said.

"Then let this moment last," he replied.

The pull between them lingered, but the cave called them back.

"I felt something else," she added. "Behind them."

"The echo?" Varg asked.

"No. A shadow mimicking the echo."

Varg's jaw tightened. "Then we're out of time."

The cave trembled, more violently this time. Dust fell like ash, and the air grew thick with the scent of brine and something sharper. The triskelion on the wall glowed faintly, its edges sharper than before, as though straining against the stone.

Runa's grip on Varg's hand tightened. "It's happening."

Varg stepped forward, positioning himself between her and the widening crack in the wall. "She's opened the path."

From the fissure, a shape emerged—not a shadow, but something worse. It bent the light around it, distorting the air like heat, moving without sound or form yet unmistakably there.

It turned toward the altar, its voice low and hollow. "I didn't know where else to go."

The words hung in the space, heavy with unspoken questions. Runa's grip on Varg's hand tightened further, her knuckles white.

"What are you?" Varg demanded, steady despite the unease rising in his voice.

The figure wavered, its edges blurred. "I don't remember," it said, voice cracking as though unaccustomed to speech.

Runa's breath caught. Something in its cadence tugged at a memory buried deep. "Who are you?" she asked, tone softer now.

"I... I don't know," it said, flickering like a dying flame. "But I remember warmth. And a voice. A voice calling me."

Varg's grip tightened. His eyes flicked to the altar. "It's manipulating you," he said, low. "Don't listen."

Runa hesitated, instincts warring with intuition. The thing didn't feel malevolent. Not entirely. But not safe, either.

"Why are you here?" she asked, her voice firmer.

"I was drawn," it said, form solidifying slightly. "By the pull. The same pull that called me here. To this place. To you."

Her chest ached with sudden, inexplicable weight. She knew that pull. Could it be another like her?

"We need to know more," she murmured. "But we must be cautious."

Varg's gaze locked on hers. "We don't have the luxury of caution. Not now."

The shape flickered again. "Please... I don't know how much longer I can hold on. I don't know what I am anymore."

Runa stepped forward, her fingers brushing the space it

occupied. "Stay," she whispered. "Just a little longer."

It paused, stabilizing slightly. "I'll try."

Runa looked to Varg, pleading. "We can't turn away someone who's lost. Not without knowing more."

His jaw clenched. But he nodded. "Then we prepare. For anything."

She turned back to the shape. "We'll help you. But you must trust us."

"Together," it echoed, barely audible.

Chapter Seven: Where Her Shadow Took Breath

Eira hadn't spoken to Zak since the chapel.

Not because she didn't want to, but because every word felt like it might give something away. A crack in her breath, a shift in her gaze, a pause between syllables—something listening might notice. It might slip through.

The silence between them wasn't angry. It was reverent. Like a shared secret, neither of them was ready to name.

But the questions were mounting.

She carried them like bones in her pocket—sharp, brittle things that rattled when she walked. What was the figure behind the mirror? Why had her mark changed again? And why did the name Runa mean something she felt, not something she understood?

On Sunday morning, Eira skipped breakfast and found herself drawn to the edge of campus, where the grounds sloped down toward the cliffs. Few students came out here. It was too exposed, too quiet. The sea beyond Glencrest was mainly obscured by mist, but today, it had cleared just enough to see the dark line of the horizon.

She sat in the grass, the cold soaking through her jeans.

The triskelion on her wrist throbbed faintly, a reminder. Her journal sat open beside her, filled with sketches and half-translated glyphs. Her eyes flicked to the last note she'd written:

The gate opens with you.

She traced the phrase slowly, then turned the page.

"You know this isn't just about you, right?"

Zak's voice behind her was calm but cut through her thoughts like wind over water.

She didn't turn. "Feels personal enough."

He sat beside her. The air between them carried the chill of salt and silence.

"It always starts that way," he said. "But it spreads. The reflection bleeds outward."

"Then why does it feel like it only wants me?"

Zak didn't answer right away. He watched the horizon with the kind of expression that had nothing to do with the weather.

"Because you were the first to answer."

Eira looked down at her wrist. "Or maybe I was just the first stupid enough to listen."

He shook his head. "No. You heard what was already inside you. That mark? It doesn't appear on people at random. It knows its way back."

Eira tilted her head. "Back to what?"

Zak hesitated. The mirrors merely mark the threshold.

She turned to him. "You said that once before. That it was something else."

"Not just a mirror. A gate. But before that... something older. Something that reflected not what you were, but who you were becoming."

Eira frowned. "Becoming? Or being taken by?"

Zak opened his notebook and flipped through pages until he landed on a drawing. It showed two circles—one above, one below—connected by three spiraling lines that formed the triskelion. But a fourth figure was drawn in faint ink this time—a shadow between both worlds.

"This," he said, tapping the center. "This is the hollow sea."

She narrowed her eyes. "What is that?"

"It's not water. Not really. It's the space between. A passage that runs between worlds. Between selves. It connects reflections."

Eira's breath caught. "Then… the thing behind the mirror… it lives in the hollow?"

Zak nodded. "It doesn't cross like we do. It pulls. Waits. Watches. Sometimes it finds a voice to echo into."

She wrapped her arms around her knees. "I keep dreaming of the woman in blue. Runa. But it feels less like dreaming now. More like… remembering."

He met her gaze. "You are."

Eira turned slowly to him.

He didn't flinch. "There's a theory. The mirror doesn't just reflect you. It recalls you. Like waking a memory, you never lived. You said her name aloud. You opened the path."

"And what about you?" she asked. "How did you find it?"

Zak's expression shifted. "I didn't. It found me when I was seven. After Sark. When I nearly drowned. I stopped breathing for two minutes. I didn't come back the same. I knew words I shouldn't have. And I remembered her."

"Runa?"

"You."

The word landed like a stone.

He looked away. "I didn't recognize your face. But I knew

the rhythm of your voice before you spoke. And the mark? It showed up when I was a teenager. Scarred in the same place. It only started glowing after you said the word."

Eira turned back to the sea. Her pulse was a distant drumbeat now.

"If I remembered something," she said, "something from a life before this one… could that explain why I've never felt like I belonged here?"

"Or why the reflection recognized you before you looked."

She stood abruptly. The wind pushed harder now, tugging at her jacket, curling fingers into her hair.

"We have to go back to the chapel," she said.

Zak stood too. "Tonight. Midnight."

This time, the chapel doors opened with less resistance, as if the building recognized them. They brought no light with them, only silence and intention.

Down the stairs, into the carved stone. The air grew colder with each step, but neither shivered.

It waited in the dark, polished and cruel.

***

Its surface shimmered like a veil suspended in breath. The symbols along the frame pulsed in a sequence. This time, the glow was not silver. It was blue.

Runa's blue.

Eira stepped forward. "What happens if we cross it?"

Zak reached into his coat and pulled a small knife. Not threatening—ritual. "Then we don't return the same."

"Were we ever the same to begin with?"

He offered the blade.

She took it.

Without hesitation, she sliced her palm. A drop of blood struck the glass, clinging to its edge. It didn't slide off.

It sank in.

The glass darkened. Swirled.

The reflection that formed was not a corridor. It was a shore. Black cliffs.

A tall woman in blue standing barefoot on wet stone.

She raised her hand. Behind her, a man stood with his staff planted in salt-worn earth.

"She sees us," Eira said.

"Then it's time."

She reached toward the glass.

It didn't feel cold.

It felt like breath.

Her fingers passed through.

Then her wrist.

Zak grabbed her free hand. "Together."

And they stepped through.

The light was dimmer on the other side, and the air heavier. The ground beneath their feet was soft with moss and memory. They stood not in a chapel but on the edge of a cliff beneath a darkened sky. The sea below churned in slow spirals, and the stars above were wrong—too many, too close, like someone had redrawn the sky by hand.

Runa stood ten feet away.

She said nothing.

Varg beside her, his staff etched with a new rune.

Eira stepped forward. The mark on her wrist burned so

brightly it illuminated her palm.

"You remember me," she said.

Runa didn't nod. She didn't have to.

She reached forward, a finger touching the mark. And whispered:

"Welcome home."

Behind them, the gate sealed.

But not before a shadow slipped through.

It didn't land.

It didn't crawl.

It hovered.

And when it finally took shape, it wore a face.

Eira's face.

It stood just behind her breath, waiting for the rhythm to slip.

Chapter Eight: Blood That Calls the Sea

The wind didn't howl. It hummed—a low, rhythmic vibration moving through the air like a pulse. Eira felt it in her chest first, then in the soles of her feet, as though the ground itself was alive. The air smelled of salt and something else, something ancient and sharp, like metal, left too long in the rain.

She stood at the edge of a cliff; the sea spread out below her, its surface a trembling green that shifted like the surface of a mirror. It wasn't water, not exactly. It moved too slowly, too deliberately, as though it were breathing.

Zak stood beside her, his hands shoved into his pockets, his shoulders tense. He hadn't said much since they'd arrived, but she could feel him watching, waiting. Zak didn't say anything, but the quiet between them felt heavy like more was on his tongue than he was ready to let out.

Up ahead, Runa and Varg moved with strange precision, their footsteps steady, yet their forms shimmered at the edges as if the world couldn't decide whether to hold onto them or let them go. They were heading for the crumbling ruins near the shore, half-swallowed by mist and time.

Eira's wrist ached—heat blooming beneath her sleeve where

the spiral still lived. She tugged her jacket closed, even though it wouldn't help. That mark wasn't just a memory but a signal—a thread tying her to something deeper, older, and still unfolding.

Her fingers brushed against it, and the pain spiked, sharp enough to make her flinch.

"It's getting stronger," she said, her voice loud enough to rise over the wind.

Zak glanced at her, his expression unreadable. "It's not just a mark, Eira. It's alive. It's connected to something."

"To what?" she asked, though she wasn't sure she wanted the answer.

He didn't respond, only looked toward the ruins.

They followed Runa and Varg down the slope, their footsteps silent on the soft earth. The ruins grew clearer as they approached, their shapes jagged and unfamiliar. The stones were etched with symbols, and the deep grooves were worn smoothly over time. Eira recognized some of them—the triskelion and the spirals—but others were foreign, their forms sharp and unsettling.

The chanting grew louder as they descended, a low, mournful sound that seemed to come from the stones themselves. It wasn't human, but it wasn't entirely alien, either. It was something in between, something that made Eira's skin crawl.

Runa stopped at the base of a cracked altar; its surface split down the middle. She turned to face them, her expression grave.

"This is where it began," she said. "The first gate. The first crossing."

Eira stepped closer, her pulse quickening. "What happened here?"

Runa's gaze was steady. "The blood stopped flowing. The door began to close. But it didn't shut completely. A name kept it alive."

"My name," Eira whispered.

Runa nodded. "Your name. Your blood. Your connection to what lies beyond."

Zak moved closer, his hand brushing Eira's arm. "What does that mean?"

Varg stepped forward, his voice low and steady. "It means you are the last of us—the last of the saltblooded. The mirror answered you because your blood remembers. It remembers the sea. It remembers the crossing."

Eira shook her head, her voice trembling. "So what? Am I supposed to stay here? Open the gate? Be some kind of key?"

Runa's expression softened. "Not a ruler, Eira. An echo. A vessel. You carry the shape of what was and can carry it forward."

Eira took a step back, her heart racing. "I didn't ask for this. I didn't ask to be part of this."

Zak moved to her side. "You don't have to do this. We can leave. Find another way."

Eira hesitated. She looked at Runa, then at Varg. Their faces were calm, but their eyes held a quiet urgency.

"What's next?" she asked, her voice barely a whisper.

Runa placed her hand on the altar. The stone began to glow, faintly at first, then brighter, until it filled the basin with light.

"You'll see," she said. "But first, you must remember."

The light surged, engulfing them. Eira closed her eyes against the brightness, but the image burned into her mind—a small, cold, and familiar room.

Her childhood bedroom.

She gasped, reaching out instinctively, but her hand met only air.

The room was the same as she remembered—the pale walls, the cracked ceiling, the small bed tucked into the corner. But it wasn't empty.

A woman stood by the window, her back to Eira. Her hair was long and dark, her posture straight and unyielding. She turned slowly, and Eira's breath caught in her throat.

The woman's face was her own. Older, sharper, but unmistakably hers.

"You're early," the woman said, her voice soft and familiar.

Eira couldn't move. Couldn't speak.

The woman stepped closer, her footsteps silent on the wooden floor. She placed something in Eira's hand—a mirror shard, its surface etched with the triskelion. It was warm, almost hot, and pulsed in time with her heartbeat.

"You were never meant to forget," the woman said. "But you had to forget to survive."

Zak's voice broke the silence. "Who are you?"

The woman tilted her head, her expression unreadable. "The one who opened the first gate. The one they called Mother."

Eira's knees buckled. Zak caught her before she fell, his grip tight on her arm.

"What are you showing me?" Eira asked, her voice barely a whisper.

The woman stepped closer, her eyes locking with Eira's. "What you were. What you could be again."

The room began to shake. The walls cracked, the floor buckled, and the air grew thick with the scent of salt and copper.

Eira screamed.

* * *

She woke on the shore, the taste of salt heavy on her lips. Runa knelt beside her, her expression unreadable.

"The memory returned."

Eira coughed, her throat raw. "She's still alive. Isn't she?"

Runa didn't answer. She didn't have to.

Zak helped her sit up, his hand steady on her back. "Is she the one who wore your face?"

Eira didn't respond. Her hand clutched the shard of glass, its surface still warm.

The sky above them began to ripple, the clouds twisting into shapes that didn't make sense.

"It's opening again," Varg said, his voice calm but urgent.

"Why?" Eira asked, her voice shaking.

Runa looked toward the horizon. "Because she knows you remember."

A low rumble filled the air, growing louder with each passing second. It wasn't just sound—it was a vibration, a presence.

"We have to seal it," Zak said, his voice tight.

Eira shook her head. "We can't. Not yet."

Varg raised his staff, his grip tight. "Then you need to choose. Stay or return. But not both."

Eira looked at the shard in her hand. It pulsed faintly, its surface glowing faintly in the dim light.

She met Zak's eyes. "I know what she wants now. And she knows what I am."

The wind surged, tearing at their clothes and pulling at their hair. The sky cracked open, sounding like bones breaking.

Something began to come through.

It didn't wear her face this time.

It wore her voice.

And when it spoke, she felt herself begin to answer.

The echo didn't stop at her lips. It moved beneath her skin, twisting and turning as though trying to find a way out.

Runa grabbed her shoulder, her grip tight. "This is not a memory anymore. This is real."

Zak stepped in front of her, his body tense. "Eira. Look at me. You're still here."

But she could barely hear him. The voice in the air was too loud, too familiar. It was her voice, but it wasn't. It was twisted, distorted, full of something dark and hungry.

"Daughter."

The word came from everywhere, echoing off the stones, the sea, and the sky.

Eira turned slowly toward the gate.

She whispered, "Mother."

And the mirror in her palm cracked.

The air stilled. The ground beneath her feet shifted like something beneath the surface had awakened.

Runa stepped back, her expression unreadable. "It's too late."

Zak didn't move. "Eira. We can still leave. We can still—"

She shook her head. "No. It's already done."

The crack split the mirror with a dry, splintering sound, like a rib giving way. Fractures bled outward in jagged threads, slicing the reflection into ruin. For a moment, the light inside flickered—a nervous, dying thing—and then it simply went out, swallowed by whatever waited on the other side.

Eira let it fall to the ground.

The air hummed again, louder this time, full of teeth and hunger.

Something was coming.

Something that knew her name.

III

Part Three: Let the One Who Speaks My Name Thrice

Let the one who dares speak my name thrice awaken that which should remain undisturbed beneath salt and stone. May their blood stir with ancient echoes, and their breath falter as the gate closes. Let the weight of their words bind them to the consequences of their call, for the slumbering shall not rise without demand, and the gate shall not remain open without sacrifice.

Chapter Nine: Diagnosis Incomplete

Zak hadn't slept in days. Not properly. When he closed his eyes, sleep didn't come as a release but as a dragging force—rough, erratic, never deep enough to bring rest. His body surrendered to it out of sheer exhaustion, but what followed wasn't peace. It was a passage. A journey through a space that felt both familiar and wrong, like walking through the echo of a place he'd once known.

The dreams were never silent.

They began in a corridor—a long, decaying hallway lined with mirrors. Some were cracked, others smudged, but all hummed faintly as though something on the other side strained to break through. And in every reflection, she waited. Not the Eira he saw daily at Glencrest, the one who tiptoed through the halls with a too-precise smile, but another version. The Eira who still bled. The one who feared.

She warned him.

Her voice was faint, fragmented, as though traveling through water. She told him things he couldn't quite understand that lingered in his mind long after waking, tangled in sweat-drenched sheets.

"She's not alone," the Eira whispered in his dreams. "The gate wasn't meant to open this way."

He didn't know what she meant, but the words clung to him, heavy and cold.

Zak had gone back, of course. After the gate had closed, after the glass conduit fell silent, he returned to the places where it had all begun. The chapel. The library. The cliffs. He wandered the empty spaces where Eira's presence still lingered, searching for something he couldn't name.

It wasn't until Eira began appearing in his dreams that he realized she hadn't come back whole.

It wasn't just trauma. It wasn't just grief.

Something else had come back with her.

Something was wearing her skin.

And no one else seemed to see it.

Except for the boy in the east wing.

The boy who'd stopped speaking the day Eira arrived at his foster home. His drawings changed after that. They were filled with spirals, three-legged symbols, and women with no faces.

The doctors called it dissociation, a neat, clinical word. It explained Eira's withdrawal, her detachment, and the way she stared at nothing for hours. It explained the water pooling beneath her bed; the symbols scratched into the walls, and the way mirrors fogged when she walked past.

But dissociation couldn't explain the chill in the air when she entered a room. It couldn't explain how her reflection sometimes blinked out of sync with her movements.

Zak knew they had missed something. Something woven too deeply into the fabric of time to show up in records or case files.

So he dug.

He found fragments, whispers of the past.

In a 1621 court record from Guernsey, he discovered a girl

named Elra Vardalok. She had Eira's face, her mark. She was accused of poisoning cattle with saltwater spells and walking through reflections. She vanished before sentencing.

In 1754, in Sark, a reverend's daughter wrote in her diary about a girl her mother had "brought home from the waves." The girl never blinked in time with her reflection.

In 1892, on the Isle of Man, a mirror was removed from the home of a grieving widower who swore his daughter had returned through it. But the girl had no pulse. She had only the shape of breath.

Zak collected every piece and pinned them to his wall. The pattern emerged slowly, inescapably.

She had been coming back repeatedly, in new bodies, through foster systems, orphanages, and churches. Each time, she lasted longer, learned more, and wore the part better.

Until now.

* * *

Eira—or the thing wearing her—sat across from him on the hill overlooking Glencrest. The air smelled faintly of burning salt.

"You've been quiet," she said.

Zak didn't answer.

She tilted her head, studying him. "Dreaming again?"

He stiffened.

"She's persistent," Eira said, her voice almost musical. "Still trying to find her way out. There's nothing left for her to reflect in."

Zak turned to face her fully. "Who are you?"

The shape of her face remained the same, but her eyes

sharpened. They were ancient, full of pity.

"I'm what remains," she said. "The marrow of what was sealed too long. She was the vessel. But she wanted answers. And the gate… it doesn't offer knowledge. Only passage."

Zak's voice cracked. "What did you do to her?"

The Eira-shape smiled. "She stayed. She chose to remember. You only survive the remembering if you're made for it."

Zak stood. "I want her back."

The thing wearing Eira's face shook its head. "You can't unopen a gate."

That night, he dreamed again.

This time, the Eira in his mind bled from her wrists, the triskelion carved deep and glowing faintly against her skin. She sat in a corridor of mirrors, their surfaces pulsing like liquid.

"They're coming for you," she said.

Zak knelt beside her. "Who?"

Her eyes filled with light. "The ones who built the gate. The ones who left it open. They want you because you helped me through."

"What do I do?" he asked.

She leaned forward, pressing her forehead to his. "Don't trust my voice."

He woke with a gasp.

And heard her humming in the next room.

In the weeks that followed, Eira was placed under psychiatric review. The state called it a precaution for her safety and the safety of others. But the air inside the hospital didn't settle. It whispered. The lights dimmed whenever she walked past. Locks jammed. Clocks lose time.

The staff wrote notes in her file: catatonic trance, transient mutism, hallucination. But they didn't know what to make of the way she stared into the glass of her meal tray, smiling as though something had smiled back.

She didn't speak for days at a time. Then she'd recite long strings of syllables no one recognized. When the on-call psychiatrist asked what language it was, she said, "Older than your questions."

Once they found her sitting in the common room, all the mirrors turned to face the walls. Her fingernails were chipped from scratching the word return into the back of a wooden chessboard. When questioned, she only whispered, "I'm not the only one they let through."

Nurses began requesting reassignment. One orderly left his shift early after finding Eira standing in the shower, fully clothed, murmuring to something in the steam.

But no one could explain why the lights flickered when she entered a room. Or why, when she sang, the windows frosted from the inside.

Then, there was Dr. Meera Lin.

She'd been reviewing Eira's file late one night, alone in the observation room. The girl hadn't spoken in three days, just sat curled on the edge of her cot, facing a bolted-down mirror that reflected only her back. Dr. Lin noted that the "regression was stable" in the file when the intercom cracked on without warning.

"She's not sleeping," a voice whispered.

Startled, Dr. Lin checked the microphone. It was off. She peered through the glass. Eira hadn't moved. But her reflection had. It stared directly back at Dr. Lin, its gaze unblinking.

Dr. Lin resigned that night. She said the girl knew her mother's name and saw something crawl out of the glass and sit beside her. No one could confirm it. The tapes played back only static.

The incident was quietly buried.

The next day, Eira spoke in a voice no one recognized. The dialect was old, strange, and guttural. She recited names, dates, the precise number of stairs leading to the hidden stone basin beneath the chapel at Glencrest, and the names of children lost to the system decades ago.

One of the nurses fainted.

Later, Eira asked if the frost would follow her home this time. Then she laughed. But only with her mouth. Her eyes stayed still.

Zak knew something had changed—not just in her, but in him.

He saw it the next time they met.

She reached for his hand, her fingers brushing his. The touch felt like ice sliding against fire. Her gaze blurred, her pupils dilating until her eyes were entirely black.

And she said, in a voice older than her body:

"You told them my name."

Zak pulled away.

She blinked. The darkness receded.

"Did I repeat something strange?" she asked, her voice soft. Almost innocent.

But the cadence was wrong. Too deliberate.

Zak began journaling every word she spoke. He matched her speech to historical records, tracing how she formed certain consonants, the pauses before vowels. He found parallels in Old Norse, Manx Gaelic, and languages nearly forgotten.

Then she called him by a name no one else knew. A nickname his grandmother had whispered in dreams. A name that had never been written down.

After that, he didn't sleep.

That night, the dream changed.

The corridor stretched further, wider. The air between the panels shimmered—cold and sticky, like wet cobwebs. Eira stood at the end, barely visible through the rippling glass.

"She knows you remember now," she said. Her mouth moved, but the voice came from behind him.

Zak turned.

Another pane of glass waited in silence.

This one didn't show his reflection—not exactly. It showed his shape, but the face was wrong. It smiled too soon and blinked too slowly. When it tilted its head, a vertebra cracked.

The real Eira cried out.

"She's using you," she said. "She's been feeding on the places you fear."

Zak asked, "Who is she?"

"She was the first voice behind the gate," Eira said. "The one who taught the sea to speak."

He stepped toward her, but the mirror pulsed.

The reflection hissed through a grin. "You shouldn't have brought her name back."

Zak woke in a sweat, his ears ringing.

Across the room, Eira stood. Silent. Still.

She tilted her head slowly.

"You were speaking in your sleep again," she said. Her lips smiled. Her eyes didn't.

He blinked.

She was gone.

But his window was open.

And written in the fog on the glass was a single word:

"Thrice."

Zak saw her less often after that. When he did, it never felt planned. She just... appeared. At the edge of a shadow. At the end of a hallway. In the corner of a photograph he didn't remember taking.

And every night, the real Eira came to him.

She looked more worn now, her eyes darker, her voice softer, like it was being pulled from far away.

"She's getting stronger," she whispered. "I don't know how long I can keep her from you."

"What does she want?" Zak asked.

"To finish what was started. To reopen the gate. And bring through what couldn't come without a name."

He reached for her, but she dissolved.

Zak awoke to scratching at his window.

There were no trees nearby.

He began to change. People noticed. His hands didn't just tremble—they jerked as if pulled by invisible threads. His speech grew disjointed, as though he was listening to another voice before responding to his thoughts. The food tasted wrong. Mirrors looked back too quickly. The air around him felt heavy with breath he hadn't drawn.

When he passed a light, he startled at his shadow, which stretched too far across the room. At times, he swore he saw ripples in the glass of the windows when no wind stirred. His journals grew more frantic, the loops in his handwriting tightening as though he was strangling his thoughts onto the page.

And inside his chest, where memory and reason should have settled, something else began to coil. A pressure. A rhythm not his own. He saw things behind people's eyes that didn't belong to them.

And always, always, that whisper:

Don't trust my voice.

He filled journals with notes. Drew maps. Traced the locations of every foster home Eira had stayed in. Each one formed a shape.

A spiral.

At the center: Glencrest.

One night, he returned to the ruins beneath the chapel. The mirror frame was cracked but not destroyed. Moss had grown in strange patterns across it. He pressed his hand to the cold metal.

The air pulsed.

Behind him, a voice said:

"She's not done yet."

He turned.

The woman standing there wore Eira's face.

But something was off. Her skin was too smooth, like stretched wax. Her eyes—Eira's eyes—held no shine, no movement, just a flat, unsettling stillness, like glass over stone. Her lips curled into a smile, too slow, too deliberate, as though remembering how to mimic one. Her head tilted at an unnatural angle, like a marionette unsure of its strings.

Zak froze.

She didn't blink.

Didn't breathe.

Didn't need to.

Chapter Ten: The Fourth Limb

The waters murmured as though they had forgotten how to speak, their whispers carrying fragments of something forgotten, something just out of reach. Eira stood at the cliff's edge, where the wind dragged itself against her skin, insistent and familiar, like a memory trying to surface. Beneath her skin, the triskelion hummed faintly, not with pain but with a rhythmic insistence, as though it were attuned to something vast and far away. She felt almost whole for the first time in days, as though her fractured parts were aligning, bone and memory clicking back into place.

The ache in her wrist lingered, but it had softened, shifting into something that felt more like resonance than pain. The horizon almost imperceptibly shifted as though it were alive, blinking slowly. Eira didn't look away.

Behind her, Varg crouched by the fire, the tip of an ancient blade stirring the embers. The metal, dull and etched with runes, glinted faintly in the shifting light, its surface alive with symbols that seemed to twist and shimmer whenever her shadow crossed them. Runa knelt beside him, weaving lengths of seaweed into small bundles, each tied around a stone. She deliberately cast them into the fire, the flames hissing as they embraced the offering.

Eira watched, her curiosity sharpening into something heavier, more urgent. "What is that?"

Runa's hands didn't pause. "Tide casting," she said, her voice low and steady. "The old way. It's how we read what wants to return."

Despite the unease coiling in her chest, Eira stepped closer, drawn to the fire. Each stone that touched the flames released a curl of steam, and as one tendril brushed her cheek, she heard it—a voice faint but unmistakable. Daughter.

She staggered back, her breath caught in her throat.

Varg's gaze didn't leave the fire. "It knows you're listening now."

Eira sat across from them, her hands gripping the cold earth to steady herself. "Tell me what's real," she said, her voice barely above a whisper. "I can't keep sorting the dreams from the waking."

Runa reached into a worn pouch at her side and pulled out a small flask made of seal hide. "Drink," she said. "It will anchor you."

Eira took the flask, her hand trembling slightly as she brought it to her lips. The liquid inside was bitter, with a sharp, metallic tang that tasted of ash, salt, and something else she couldn't name. Her stomach recoiled, but her mind sharpened, the fog lingering at the edges of her thoughts dissipating.

Varg's voice, when it came, was low and deliberate. "There's a reason the gate chose you," he said. "And a reason you didn't break when you crossed. You carry the original bloodline—one that remembers too much."

Eira stared into the fire, its flames steady and unwavering. "What is she?" she asked, her voice barely audible. "The one who came back with me?"

Runa didn't answer right away. She cast the last stone into the fire, and the flames flared black this time, dark, oily smoke rising into the air.

"She's not one thing," Runa said quietly. "She's what was left behind the first time. When the sea spoke, and the gate cracked."

Varg lifted the blade, pressing it flat against the ground. The runes along its surface shimmered faintly, like breath on a cold morning.

"She was never supposed to find a name," he said. "But the world kept calling her back. Through women who looked like you. Through songs forgotten. Through cracks in mirrors."

Eira pressed a hand to her chest, her fingers curling into the fabric of her shirt. "She's inside me."

Runa met her gaze, her expression unwavering. "No," she said. "She's beside you. For now. But the longer she's near, the easier it will be for her to become you."

Eira closed her eyes, the corridor from her dreams pressing against her eyelids, pulsing like a heartbeat. Her body shivered though no wind stirred the air.

"How do we stop her?" she asked.

Varg's voice was steady, unyielding. "You don't," he said. "You walk deeper into her shadow until you find where she buried herself."

That night, they descended into the caves beneath the cliffs, the air growing colder and heavier with each step. Eira walked barefoot, and the wet stone beneath her feet reminded her that she was still alive and tethered to the present. The torch Varg carried cast long, liquid shadows against the walls, their flickering forms twisting into shapes that seemed to move of their own accord. Ancient markings wound their way through the stone—triskelions, spirals, claw-like sigils. One image carved deep into the rock caught her eye: a woman with no face, her arms too long, her fingers tapering into points that seemed to curl inward.

Runa ran her fingers along the carving, her touch reverent. "These were warnings, once," she said. "Now they're just forgotten."

Eira's voice was barely a whisper. "She's been here."

Runa nodded. "Before you. Before me. Before the islands were named."

They reached a cavern where the air thickened and tasted metallic and sharp, like wet iron. In the center of the space stood a mirror—not glass or metal, but something in between. It rippled faintly, its surface alive, shifting like water under breath.

Runa stepped back, her voice low. "This is the original one. The first gate. The one she came through."

Eira approached slowly, her reflection wavering on the surface. It didn't mimic her movements; instead, it smiled before she did.

"She remembers this place," Eira said, her voice wrong—just enough to make her pause.

Varg laid the runeblade across her shoulders, its weight grounding her. Runa began to chant, her voice low and guttural, the sounds bending into shapes that didn't belong to any living language.

The mirror hummed in response, its surface rippling more urgently. Eira stepped closer, her mark burning hot against her skin. She hesitated for only a moment before placing her hand on the surface.

She half-expected resistance, the cold, hard rejection of glass or metal. Instead, the surface yielded beneath her touch, warm and pliant, like flesh. It gave way with a slow, unsettling pulse, as though it had been waiting for her all along.

Her body slipped through.

She stood in the corridor again, but this time, it was alive.

Mirrors lined both sides, each one reflecting a version of her. Some were younger, some older. One was burned, her skin cracked and blistered. Another was blind, her eyes milky and unseeing. One held a child she didn't recognize, its small hands gripping her shirt.

And then came the last mirror.

* * *

This reflection didn't move. It stared, unblinking, her face looking back at her, but wrong. The eyes were empty, not lifeless, but vacant, as though something else had taken residence behind them, turning the lights on without knowing how to look out. There was no recognition, no tether to the body that wore them—just stillness, watching, like a mirror left too long in the dark.

Behind it, a shape moved.

Not fast. Not slow. Intentional.

A woman.

Tall, her hair floating around her like seaweed in water. Her eyes were the color of dead coral, pale and empty.

"I gave you my name," she whispered. "You made it yours. Now let me breathe."

Eira tried to run, but the corridor tilted beneath her, the ground shifting like liquid. Glass shattered somewhere behind her, the sound sharp and final. She fell to her knees, the pain blooming in her chest, sharp and insistent.

The figure knelt before her, her face inches from Eira's.

"You opened the gate with your blood," she said, her voice soft and cruel. "You crossed because I let you. But you kept the name. That was never yours."

Eira screamed, "Take it back, then!"

The woman grinned, her mouth widening unnaturally, cracking at the edges like wax stretched too far. "Oh, I will."

Her fingers pressed into Eira's chest, passing through flesh like water. She found something, pulled—

Pain bloomed, sharp and unbearable.

But Eira reached too.

Her hand closed around the woman's wrist, and the corridor exploded with light—searing, absolute, a rupture in reality itself. The sound that followed wasn't just brightness; it was sound, a thousand voices overlapping into a single, untranslatable scream. The mirrors cracked, and a chorus of splintering glass shook the corridor to its core. Eira's vision fractured into bursts of color and memory—cold saltwater, heatless flame, the lull of lullabies in tongues she didn't know she knew. Her body shuddered, not just from pain but dislocation, as if her skin no longer remembered where to belong.

Then, silence.

A terrible, pressurized silence that settled into her lungs like ash.

Eira gasped, her body arching off the stone floor as if expelled from another world. Her hand was still outstretched, trembling, blood pooling in her palm like a mark made fresh. The cavern felt louder than before—the water's drip echoed like drumbeats, and her breath rattled in her throat like wind scraping bone.

For a moment, she couldn't speak. Her eyes fluttered open and caught the low shimmer of mist curling around her fingers, retreating slowly like something disappointed not to have stayed. Her chest ached as if something inside had been carved and stitched backward.

When she sat up, she didn't look at the others. She looked at the spot where the mirror had been—only it hadn't just vanished.

It had fled. The mirror was gone. Only a shimmer of mist remained.

Runa leaned over her, but didn't speak right away. Her breath hitched. Her eyes tracked the shimmer where the mirror had been, and she crossed herself in an old way—two fingers pressed against her throat. Then, slowly, as if afraid her voice might summon something, she said, "You brought something back, didn't you?"

Eira nodded slowly.

Her palm was red with blood. But the triskelion had changed. A fourth arm had begun to grow.

Varg stepped forward, holding a scroll he had unearthed from the stone. It was written in bone ink, words from the first tongue.

"It says the fourth path awakens the Mother."

Eira blinked. "Mother?"

Runa turned pale. "The origin. Not a person. A force. She's what watches the mirrors. The voice behind the voice."

Eira tried to stand, but the cavern shook.

A wind howled from beneath them.

And something called her name.

It echoed not in the air, but inside her chest, like a heartbeat that didn't belong to her.

But it wasn't her voice that answered.

It was the thing wearing her face, tilting its head—vertebrae cracking with the motion—its lips opening in a gesture not of speech, but the memory of speech. Something far colder than a smile.

Then it moved.

Not walking—sliding. Too smooth to be natural. Like a memory trying to imitate life.

Eira staggered back, nearly toppling over the slick cavern stone. Her mark burned beneath her wrist, and heat seeped up her arm like molten thread. Runa shouted something behind her, but it was drowned out by the sudden stillness—an unnatural silence that pressed against the bones.

The creature's lips parted.

"She wakes."

Zak stepped forward without thinking, his blade already drawn, but the thing didn't move—not even a twitch. Instead, it turned, slowly, deliberately, not to face him but to look back at the space where the mirror had once been. The shimmer reappeared, faint at first, like heat rising off pavement. Then it changed. It started to bleed—no blood, but something was leaking through, a slow, steady fracture opening in the air itself, as if the world was beginning to split at the seams.

Through it, they glimpsed something vast.

Not a body. Not a being. A presence.

Eyes—hundreds, suspended in the dark like fish caught in oil. A single limb, shaped like smoke, brushed against reality's edges.

The fracture widened.

And from within came a whisper—no, a rustle, like pages turning underwater.

Runa collapsed to her knees, blood at her ears.

"Mother," the creature said. Not with reverence. With hunger.

Eira screamed as her legs buckled. The triskelion on her wrist shimmered violently, the fourth limb fully formed—and moving.

Zak lunged forward, grabbed her, pulled her back as the shimmer in the air surged forward, becoming a mouth without teeth, opening wide—

And swallowing the creature whole.

The light snapped shut.

Silence followed.

But deep beneath the cavern floor, something began to breathe—slow and vast, like lungs the size of caverns expanding for the first time in centuries. It was a breath that carried dust from ages forgotten, stirring stone and soil with every rise. It was not alive like flesh but remembered life and hungered for form.

And somewhere, in the dark, the Mother began to stir.

*　*　*

When the light vanished, the emulate was gone. The cavern was empty.

The air still trembled from whatever had passed through, but Eira was no longer there.

Not entirely.

Back at Glencrest, the world had carried on. Evening light filtered through the windows of the dormitory halls, soft and honeyed, unaware of what had unraveled beneath the earth. But in Room 3B, everything had stopped.

Zak was the one who found her.

He checked on her after she failed to respond to his texts—unusual, even for her. The door was unlocked. Her light was on.

She sat perfectly still at the edge of her bed, her hands folded neatly in her lap, eyes open but unfocused, staring at the opposite wall as if watching something no one else could see.

At first, he thought she was deep in thought. Maybe meditating, or lost in one of her dissociative fogs. But she didn't blink. She didn't move. Not even when he called her name.

Her breathing was shallow—barely perceptible. Her skin had gone pale beneath the light, but not like illness—more like absence. Like the blood itself had receded.

He touched her shoulder.

It was like touching stone.

Cold. Still.

Not lifeless… but emptied.

Her lips were parted, slightly, as if she had been about to speak and simply… stopped.

Zak stayed with her for nearly an hour before help arrived. He didn't speak. He just watched her, terrified she might suddenly blink—or worse, smile.

When the Glencrest staff arrived, they whispered words like *catatonia* and *unresponsive episode* and *dissociative fugue*. But no one could explain the faint marks beginning to show beneath her skin—spirals, almost bruises, blooming like memory just under the surface.

They called for an emergency transfer.

By nightfall, she was on her way to Saint Amaranth, wrists wrapped gently in gauze, eyes still fixed on nothing.

And in her dorm room, long after the doors had closed behind her, the mirror above her dresser fogged from within. Then came a sound—small, soft, but deliberate.

A knock.

Chapter Eleven: Echogate

The passage of time at Saint Amaranth was impossible to measure. Days melted into one another; their edges blurred as watercolors left too long in the rain. Eira had spent seven months within its sterile walls, but the sameness of the place made it feel endless. The lights hummed faintly, never dimming; the air smelled perpetually of antiseptic and plastic, clinging to her skin long after she showered. The walls were an unbroken expanse of white, interrupted only by muted paintings or clocks that didn't tick. Even the floors were designed to soften the sound, swallowing footsteps and muffling the world.

The mirror in her room was shatterproof, sealed behind a layer of thick plexiglass. It hung directly across from her bed, its surface smooth and cold. At first, it reflected only what it saw—Eira's tired gaze, her unruly hair, the pale blue scrubs they gave her to wear. But over time, the reflection began to change. Subtle at first: a delay, a fraction of a second too slow to match her movements. Then it lingered when she turned away, as though it were watching her.

The therapists called it a trauma response. They labeled it disassociation, night terrors, anything to fit it into a neat little box they could treat. But Eira knew better. She wasn't slipping away from herself.

She was slipping into something else.

The first time it happened, she didn't scream. She didn't gasp or struggle. She blinked, and in that blink, she was no longer tethered to her body. Instead, she watched herself from above, floating near the ceiling, looking down at her own form sprawled across the bed. Her chest rose and fell to a rhythm that wasn't hers. And in the corner of the room, something else stood—something that wore her shape with unsettling precision.

Saint Amaranth's staff prided themselves on compassion. They wore it like a uniform: rehearsed smiles, soft voices, carefully chosen words meant to soothe. Therapists spoke of trust and healing, of reintegration and processing. Everything about the facility was designed to comfort, to contain, to control.

But Ava didn't follow their script.

Ava had been at Saint Amaranth long before Eira arrived. Thin and pale, with dark hair that hung limply around her shoulders, she moved through the corridors like a ghost. Her eyes never met yours, always drifting just past your shoulder, as though she were watching something no one else could see. And she hummed—a low, tuneless sound that vibrated in the air, unsettling and heavy.

Their rooms were across from each other. During group sessions, Ava rarely spoke unless prompted, and even then, her words came out wrong, as though they belonged to someone else entirely.

"Some mirrors only show what's missing," she said once, her voice barely audible.

Another time, she looked directly at Eira and said, "My

reflection remembers more than I do."

The staff diagnosed her with early-onset schizophrenia, delusional disorder—anything to explain away the things she saw and said. But Eira recognized something in Ava's words. Not madness, but knowing.

One night, Eira found Ava kneeling by the hallway window, her forehead pressed against the glass, whispering to something Eira couldn't see.

"Do you see it too?" Eira asked, her voice barely louder than Ava's murmuring.

Ava didn't flinch. "Not always," she said. "But it sees me."

Later, Eira would think of that moment as a turning point—not a warning, but an invitation. A hand on her shoulder in a burning room.

The mirror in Eira's room stopped reflecting her entirely during her third week at Saint Amaranth. She tested it, turning her head sharply, raising her left hand instead of her right, forcing a grin that felt unnatural. Each time, the reflection hesitated, lagging behind by a breath, a blink, a heartbeat. It was subtle, something the cameras wouldn't catch, but Eira felt it.

It wasn't trying to match her anymore.

It was watching her.

The smile in the mirror didn't reach its eyes.

Eira began covering the mirror with a towel at night, telling herself it was to help her sleep. But sleep didn't come. Instead, the dreams returned.

Corridors. Always corridors. Lined with mirrors. Lined with versions of herself.

Some were younger, their eyes wide and uncomprehending. Others were older, their faces lined with weariness and something that looked like regret. One bled from her eyes, tears of red tracing paths down her cheeks. Another mouthed Eira's name with cracked lips, her voice a dry whisper that Eira felt more than heard.

She didn't walk in those dreams. She observed. She watched herself walk, her reflections moving through the corridors with purpose, their footsteps echoing in sync.

Ava disappeared on a Tuesday.

No goodbyes. No notes. Just gone.

The staff said she had been transferred. But her shoes were still tucked beneath her bed, and her worn paperback journal—filled with spirals, runes, and fragmented phrases— was nowhere to be found. No one saw her leave. The cameras showed nothing unusual.

Eira asked around, cautiously at first, then more directly.

"She was unstable," a nurse told her with a shrug. "Sometimes that accelerates discharge."

But the hallway felt emptier without Ava's humming. Too quiet. Too still.

That night, Eira dreamed of her again. Ava stood barefoot in the corridor, her mouth slightly open, her eyes black and unseeing.

"You're not the first door," she whispered. "But you might be the last."

The next morning, someone had scratched spirals into the surface of Eira's tray. Not her. Not anyone with fingernails like hers. But the marks were deep, jagged, and too precise to be accidental. The nurses dismissed it as a dishwasher malfunction.

Dr. Halvorsen, the head psychiatrist, declared Eira's progress "textbook."

"She's stable," he told the board. "She's accepted her past. She's compliant with medication. Her symptoms are in complete remission."

They didn't ask about the symbols reappearing on her ceiling in permanent marker. They didn't question the way her vital signs dropped to near-zero every night between 2:00 and 2:15 a.m., only to stabilize moments later. They didn't notice that her reflection had stopped blinking entirely.

On her last night at Saint Amaranth, Eira stood barefoot in the dim glow of her bathroom. The door was cracked just enough to let in a sliver of yellow light from the hallway. She hadn't turned on the tap, but the mirror fogged as though someone—or something—had been breathing on the other side. She wiped it with the edge of her sleeve, her hand steady despite the tightness in her chest.

Her reflection stared back.

Behind it, Ava stood.

Her eyes were wrong—too dark, too empty—and her mouth hung open slightly, as though she were about to speak. But it wasn't Ava's voice that filled Eira's mind. It was a presence, vast and cold, pressing against the edges of her thoughts.

"Let her go," Eira said, her voice steady.

Ava didn't respond. But the mirror pulsed beneath Eira's palm, a slow, insistent rhythm that matched the beat of her heart.

And then Ava was gone. Only the reflection remained.

But the eyes staring back weren't hers.

The next morning, they handed her a duffel bag filled with her old clothes and a plastic cup of pills she palmed and slipped into her sock. They told her she'd been approved for release, that her integration had been a success.

The air outside hit her like a slap.

* * *

Zak turned eighteen while Eira was gone—months after the morning he found her in her room at Glencrest, completely still. Not asleep, not unconscious—just… absent. Her eyes were open, unfocused, locked on something no one else could see. She didn't blink. Didn't speak. Just stood there, like time had forgotten to carry her forward. The staff said she was in shock, that trauma could freeze a person like that. But Zak knew better. The air had changed in that room. The mirror behind her was humming.

After they took her to Saint Amaranth, Glencrest went on like it always had—drab routines, muted conversations, and locked doors that didn't always stay quiet. But for Zak, something had broken loose. The place felt thinner, like the walls were no longer holding the world back—just barely keeping it from spilling in.

He didn't have anyone waiting for him on the other side. His file listed Lars Macrae as his contact—a name from the distant edges of his childhood. Lars had been a quiet presence, sending notes and packages once in a while. A compass. A pocketknife. A postcard with no return address. But they hadn't spoken since the gate closed, since Eira stopped being Eira.

When the paperwork came through on his birthday, he signed it without hesitation. Eighteen meant choice. And he chose to leave. No fanfare, no warning. Just a backpack with the bare essentials: a few of Eira's sketches, his tattered journal, and the small broken pieces he always kept wrapped in cloth.

He walked out just after dusk. The sky was the color of old bruises. The wind carried nothing familiar. And as the gates shut behind him, Glencrest didn't groan or sigh or call out his name. It simply let him go.

Because whatever had tied him to that place wasn't in the walls anymore.

It had already followed her. He knew he had to get her out before all was lost.

Zak was waiting in the parking lot, leaning against the car. His eyes were tired, his expression unreadable. He hadn't seen her since the gate closed.

She got in without speaking.

The engine hummed to life. The tires crunched over gravel.

He glanced at her in the rearview, and she looked up at the exact moment.

For just a second—less than a blink—her lips curled into a smile. But her eyes stayed still, flat and unreadable.

Zak looked again.

She was staring out the window, her face calm, her expression unreadable.

"I thought they'd keep you longer," he said.

"They tried," she murmured.

Silence stretched between them, heavy and thick.

"They said I'm better," she added.

Zak's knuckles whitened on the steering wheel. "Are you?"

Eira turned her head slowly, her gaze meeting his.

"I'm not the one asking."

That night, at a roadside motel two hours outside Glencrest, Eira sat on the edge of the bed, her knees pulled to her chest. Across from her, bolted to the far wall, was a full-length mirror, its edges tarnished, its surface etched with faint, unreadable symbols. The manufacturer's logo had long since faded, leaving behind only the ghost of letters in a language that shouldn't exist.

It cracked the moment she stepped in front of it. The sound wasn't loud—more like a shift in pressure, soft and internal, as if something inside her had snapped. A hairline fracture crept across the surface, delicate as a blood vessel just beneath the skin.

Her breath caught and held.

It then began to murk over.

She hadn't touched the faucet. There was no humidity in the room.

She stepped closer, reaching out with trembling fingers.

Her hand met the glass surface and felt—warmth. Not heat, but breath. Like the space between two mouths before a kiss. She recoiled instinctively, but her eyes stayed fixed on the glass.

The reflection blinked first.

And then it spoke.

Not aloud. The words pressed directly into her mind, a low, insistent presence.

"You left the door open."

A handprint formed in the center of the mirror. Too long. Too wide. The fingertips smeared downward, as though something on the other side was trying to hold on.

Another voice joined in—Ava's. Quiet. Painful.

"I didn't mean to let her in."

The glass shimmered. Eira's body tensed.

She stepped back, but the reflection didn't follow her movement. It tilted its head, examining her with an unnerving calm, like a scientist studying a specimen pinned beneath glass.

Zak knocked twice on the adjoining door before stepping into the room.

"You okay?" he asked, his voice casual, but his eyes scanned her too quickly.

She turned to face him, her expression neutral. "I'm not tired."

He stepped farther into the room. "You haven't slept since we left."

She didn't respond.

He noticed the mirror then. The crack. The handprint.

"Was that there before?" he asked.

She shrugged. "It doesn't matter."

Zak hesitated. "You're not the same."

She turned to him, her movements slow and measured. "I wasn't supposed to be."

Her voice held no malice—only memory.

The light in the room flickered. Inside it was her reflection sharpened, just for a second. It wasn't her at all. It was something else, wearing her outline, its grin too wide, its eyes too still.

Zak didn't speak. He just nodded slowly, his skin prickling with cold.

She moved past him toward the window and stared out at the darkened parking lot. Her breath fogged the glass.

Behind her, the mirror pulsed again.

And this time, it whispered one word—low and final.

"Soon."

Zak didn't sleep. He lay awake, staring at the ceiling, listening to the quiet groan of the pipes and the uneven rhythm of her breathing across the room. But even in the dark, he couldn't shake the feeling that it wasn't Eira breathing.

She didn't move.

Neither did her reflection.

And when the morning light finally touched the mirror's surface, the handprint was gone. But a new mark had formed in its place, faint and almost hidden in the tarnish.

Three spirals.

And beneath them—

One word.

"Home."

Then a knock. Not from the door. From inside the mirror. Just one. A tap. Hollow.

As though something was testing the barrier again.

Eira stirred but didn't wake.

Outside, in the faint blue haze of dawn, the motel's neon sign sputtered—on, off, on. The air was still. But in the reflection of the window, there was movement.

Not Eira.

Not Zak.

Something behind them.

It lingered in the shimmering glass, a silhouette barely visible—a shape not made for this world but pushing through anyway.

The knock came again.

This time, it wasn't hollow.

It echoed.

Then, silence. Not the stillness of peace, but the tense breath held before something terrible fills the void. Zak sat up, his body alert despite the exhaustion threading his limbs. He scanned the dim room, his eyes moving from the mirror to the bed to the silhouette of Eira beneath the blanket. She hadn't moved—not an inch.

But her reflection had.

In the mirror, she was standing now.

Facing him.

The blanket on the bed was undisturbed.

Zak's throat went dry. He reached slowly for the bedside lamp, his heart stuttering. The bulb sparked and fizzled out the second he touched the switch.

The mirror darkened.

The reflection smiled.

And it began to move toward him—slowly, like a predator stalking prey across a stretch of dream. Behind it, the glass stretched and breathed like skin.

He stumbled backward, knocking over the lamp. His chest rose and fell in uneven bursts, panic laced with confusion. "Eira?" he whispered. "Eira, wake up."

But the girl in the bed didn't stir.

The reflection cocked its head.

And then it spoke—not with sound, but a pressure against his mind, like cold fingers pushing words into his skull.

"Don't you see it now?"

Zak fell to his knees, hands clamped over his ears as if the gesture could hold the voice out.

"I see you," it whispered.

The mirror flared. A blinding flash of light spilled into the room, bleaching everything colorless. When it dimmed, the reflection was gone.

But Eira stood barefoot by the window.

She didn't speak. Just stared at the mirror, her eyes unreadable.

Behind her, on the glass, new spirals had formed. Smaller. Nesting.

Like eggs.

Zak found his voice shaky and uneven. "What's happening?"

She didn't answer. She placed a hand over the center spiral and exhaled—a long, measured breath.

The mirror didn't crack this time.

It opened.

A layer peeled away at its center, exposing a darkness beyond it. It was not empty, not silent, but full of rustling things, breathing things, and watching things.

Eira turned to Zak, her expression soft, almost kind. "I think it's time I went back."

He stood, reaching out, panicked. "You don't have to—"

But her fingers had already found the seam.

She stepped through.

The mirror sealed behind her.

Zak was alone in the room, staring at his pale face in the now-perfect reflection. No cracks. No spirals.

Just stillness.

And then, in the faintest shimmer, the reflection of Eira flinched.

Then she started to laugh.

Chapter Twelve: Ash of the First Child

The motel room was silent, but it wasn't the kind of silence that brought peace. It was the kind that settled like a weight, pressing down on your chest until it became hard to breathe. Zak stood near the edge of the bed, his hands shoved deep into his jacket pockets, staring at the panel on the far wall. It was just a piece of glass—ordinary, unremarkable, the kind you'd find in any cheap motel. But he couldn't shake the feeling that it was watching him.

The surface was smooth, reflecting the dim light from the flickering neon sign outside. The walls were stained a pale yellow from years of cigarette smoke, and the air smelled faintly of mildew and old carpet. Everything about the room screamed temporary, a place people came to forget or be forgotten. But Zak wasn't here to ignore. He was here because Eira had been here. After all, this was where she had stood just hours before, staring into that same polished surface.

He could still see her in his mind, her reflection pale and drawn, her eyes hollow as she reached to touch the glass. He had watched her step through it, her body vanishing as though the surface had swallowed her whole. There had been no resistance, no hesitation. Just a quiet breath, and then she was gone.

The air in the room felt thinner now, as if something vital had been pulled away with her. Zak couldn't shake the feeling that the glass was different, too. It looked the same—flat, lifeless—but there was a subtle vibration he couldn't place. It was as if the surface held its breath, waiting for something to happen.

Zak pulled Eira's notebook from his pocket. It was small, bound in worn black leather, which she had carried everywhere. He had found it on the floor by the bed, as if she had dropped it in her hurry to leave. The pages were filled with her frantic sketches, her notes scrawled in the margins, half-finished thoughts that bent into each other. But now, as he flipped through it, the pages were blank. All except one.

At the very back, a single line stared up at him, the ink still wet:

"Runa is awake."

Zak closed the notebook, his chest tightening. He didn't need to reread it. He knew what it meant. Runa had been the one to set everything in motion, the one who had tied Eira to the gateways, to the thing that had followed her back. And now she was awake.

The air in the room shifted, and Zak felt it before he saw it—a subtle vibration, like the echo of a sound that shouldn't exist. The glass pulsed faintly as if something on the other side was pressing against it.

He didn't want to look but couldn't tear his eyes away.

The surface undulated like water disturbed by a stone. Zak's reflection wavered, then twisted into something unfamiliar. His face stretched, his eyes hollowed, and for a moment, he saw himself as he might look years from now—tired, broken, haunted.

The reflection grinned. Not with Zak's mouth but with

something else. Something that didn't belong.

"You know what's coming," it said, the voice low and soft, almost kind.

Zak's throat tightened. He wanted to look away, smash the glass, do anything but listen. But he couldn't move.

* * *

"You've always known," the reflection continued. "You've felt it. The pull. The weight of it. You've been waiting for this, even if you didn't realize it."

"That's not true," Zak muttered, but the words felt hollow.

The reflection's grin widened. "Isn't it? You've been helping her. You've been guiding her. You've known all along what she was, what she could do. And you didn't stop it."

Zak's hand tightened around the notebook. "I was trying to help her."

"Were you?" the reflection asked, its voice almost pitying. "Or were you helping yourself? Trying to fill the emptiness you've carried for so long?"

The room felt colder. Zak's chest ached, a dull, throbbing pain that spread through him like a slow leak. He didn't want to believe it, but the words settled into him, heavy and true. He had been helping Eira, but also searching for something—a way to fill the void that had been with him for as long as he could remember.

The surface shimmered again, and the reflection changed. This time, it wasn't Zak staring back. It was Runa.

Her eyes were dark, hollow, and ancient. She looked tired, as though she had been carrying the weight of centuries on her shoulders.

"You can't run from this, Zak," she said. Her voice was calm, but there was an edge to it, a quiet urgency that made his skin crawl. "You've been part of this for longer than you know. You've seen what's coming. You've felt it in your bones."

Zak shook his head. "I don't understand."

"You don't have to," Runa replied. "Not yet. But you will. And when you do, you'll have to make a choice."

The glass went dark. Zak staggered back, his heart racing. He wanted to scream, break something, and make the feeling of frustration disappear. But he couldn't move. He was frozen between the reflection and the truth it had shown him.

The air in the room grew heavier, pressing down on him. He couldn't breathe. He couldn't think. All he could do was stand there, staring at the panel, waiting for it to show him something else.

But it didn't. It was just a mirror again. Silent. Still.

Zak sank to the floor, his back against the bed. He closed his eyes, trying to steady his breathing. He wanted to forget what he had seen, to pretend it was just a dream, a trick of the light. But he couldn't. The truth was lodged in his mind like a splinter he couldn't dig out.

He had helped Eira. He had guided her. And now, he had to face the consequences.

Runa was awake.

And she was coming.

Zak didn't know how long he sat there, staring at the blank pages of Eira's notebook. The silence in the room was suffocating, broken only by the faint hum of the neon sign outside. He couldn't shake the feeling that he was being watched, that something was lingering just beyond the edge of his vision, waiting for him to let his guard down.

He thought about Eira and how she had looked at him before she stepped through the glass. There had been no fear in her eyes, only determination. She knew what she was doing and did it anyway. Zak had tried to stop her, but deep down, he knew it was too late. She had already made her choice.

He thought about the first time he had seen her, standing in the shadows of Glencrest Academy, her eyes scanning the crowd as if she were searching for something. He had recognized something in her that felt familiar, even though he couldn't place it. They were two pieces of the same puzzle, broken apart and scattered across time.

And now, she was gone.

Zak closed his eyes, trying to steady his breathing. He couldn't afford to fall apart now. Not when there was still so much at stake. He had to find her and figure out what had happened to her. But first, he needed answers.

He opened his eyes and stared at the reflective surface again. It was just a mirror, nothing more. But he couldn't shake the feeling that it was waiting for something—and was holding its breath, just like he was.

Zak stood up, his legs unsteady. He walked over to the panel, his reflection wavering in the dim light. He hesitated for a moment, then pressed his hand against the glass.

It was cold, unnaturally so. The surface felt smooth, almost slippery, like touching the surface of a still pond. Zak's heart raced as he pressed harder, his fingers trembling.

For a moment, nothing happened. And then, slowly, the surface began to ripple.

Zak's reflection wavered, then twisted into something unfamiliar. His face stretched, his eyes hollowed, and for a moment, he saw himself as he might look years from now—tired, broken, haunted.

The reflection smirked. Not with Zak's mouth, but with something else's. Something that didn't belong.

"You can't escape it, Zak," it said, the voice low and soft. "You've been part of this for too long. You've seen too much. And now, it's time to face the truth."

Zak tried to pull his hand away, but his fingers wouldn't move. They were stuck, as if the glass held him, pulling him in.

"Let me go," he said, his voice strained.

The reflection's expression deepened. "I can't do that, Zak. You're already part of this. You've always been part of this. And now, it's time to finish what you started."

The air in the room grew colder, pressing down on him like a weight. Zak tried to scream, but no sound came out. His chest tightened, and his vision blurred. He couldn't breathe. He couldn't think. All he could do was stand there, trapped between the reflection and the truth it showed him.

And then, just as suddenly as it had started, it stopped. The surface went still, the ripples fading away. Zak's reflection returned, pale and shaken.

He stumbled back, his heart racing. He didn't know what had just happened, but he knew one thing: he couldn't stay here. He had to find Eira. He had to figure out what was happening before it was too late.

Zak grabbed his jacket and headed for the door. As he stepped out into the cool night air, he couldn't shake the feeling that something was following him, watching him. He didn't know what was waiting for him, but he knew one thing: he couldn't turn back now.

Because Runa was awake.

And she was coming.

IV

Part Four: The Mouth of Mirrors

The tide takes more than it returns.
It remembers the shape of the ones it lost.
It calls back not the body but the breath that lived
inside the body. First, it is hollow, then it is hungry.
There are gates older than memory.
Older than grief.
And when the last gate opens, it will not be to another
world.
It will be what remains between them.

Chapter Thirteen: Where the Salt Remembers Blood

The motel unraveled behind him, its lights dimming one by one as though swallowing their own glow. Zak didn't look back. He couldn't trust the space behind him, not with the air pressed against his chest or the way the gravel seemed to shift underfoot, as though the ground was breathing. Every step felt like wading through something unseen, a weight around his ankles; a whisper lodged too deep in his mind to shake loose.

The fields ahead dissolved into salt marshes, their edges blurred and uncertain. Beyond them, the sea lay flat and black, unbroken by the faintest glimmer of a horizon. Salt and time had hollowed out the land here, leaving only dead grasses and the skeletal remains of fences—a place that had given up pretending to be alive.

The stars hung low, too close, their shapes unfamiliar. Zak didn't try to make sense of them. They weren't constellations anymore. They looked like raw and jagged wounds as if the sky was unraveling.

He wasn't sure when he first noticed her.

She didn't call out.

She didn't move.

She stood at the edge where the salt flats gave way to deeper marshland, a figure so still that she might have been a trick of the dark.

Eira.

Or the thing that had taken her place.

Her feet were bare, caked with mud and salt. Her arms hung loose, her hair clinging to her shoulders like seaweed dragged ashore. Her face held enough of Eira to hurt—the line of her jaw and shoulders curved—but her eyes gave her away. They were too empty, too ancient. No flicker of fear, no hint of recognition. They were as still as the tide before it pulled back to drown the shore.

Zak stopped twenty feet away. The wind off the sea carried the tang of rust and decay, sharp enough to make his throat tighten. His mouth tasted like old pennies.

She tilted her head just enough to suggest curiosity.

"You shouldn't have followed," she said.

Her voice was almost right. Almost.

Zak's hands curled into fists. The mark on his wrist—the spiral—throbbed once, a slow and deliberate pulse beneath his skin.

"You left the door open," he said, his voice hoarse.

She smiled. Not a real smile—a deliberate and cold adjustment of her lips.

"Not for you."

Behind her, the ground stirred.

Zak didn't blink. Didn't dare to breathe. The bog shifted, mounds of Earth rising and falling like something trying to wake. Bulges formed in the mud were too uneven to be human and too deliberate to be natural. Faces pushed to the surface, collapsing inward as quickly as they appeared, their features smeared and broken. Limbs stretched out, too long, too thin, dragging trails of brackish water as they sank back into the mire.

The salt of the land groaned a low, mournful sound that seemed to come from everywhere.

The Earth split open.

And from it, a second, Eira pulled herself free.

This one was wrong.

Her skin hung in tatters, revealing glistening bone beneath. Her mouth gaped open in a silent scream, her jaw unhinged and stretched too far. The triskelion burned across her chest, its shape distorted, the fourth arm twisting upward into a tight, clenched fist.

Zak stumbled back, his boots slipping in the mire.

The first Eira—the one wearing her skin—watched him. Amused. Patient.

"They're hungry," she said. "They've been waiting for the mirror to forget its shape."

Zak's chest tightened. He remembered Runa's voice, steady and low, her words echoing in his mind like a warning.

"Not everything that waits is dead."

***

He pressed his palm against the spiral on his wrist. It burned, but he welcomed the pain. It anchored him, kept him from sinking into the ground that seemed to pull at him with every step.

"You don't have to be this," he said, trembling.

The girl tilted her head.

"I am this."

The soil behind her stirred again. Dozens of shapes rose from the mud, their forms twisted and incomplete. Some dragged themselves forward with limbs that bent in too many places. Others stayed still, their outlines barely human, their bodies draped in seaweed and broken shells. They didn't move toward him, but their presence filled the air, suffocating, hungry.

Zak's legs ached to run. His chest felt tight, his pulse pounding in his ears.

Instead, he stepped forward.

The real Eira—the one buried beneath the thing wearing her skin—was still there. He had to believe that. Without that belief, he was lost.

"You aren't finished yet," he said, his voice steady despite the fear clawing at his throat.

The thing wearing Eira's skin smiled wider. Her teeth were sharper now, too perfect. They looked like they could cut through more than flesh.

"You're right," she whispered. "I'm just beginning."

The Earth erupted.

Not with fire or wind, but with life—if it could be called that. Figures clawed their way free from the mud, their movements jerky and unnatural. Some screamed silently, their mouths open in soundless wails. Others dragged themselves forward, their bodies snapping into grotesque shapes as they moved. One lunged at Zak, its jaw unhinging so wide it split the skin at the corners. Another reached out, its fingers leaving streaks of frost on the air.

Zak tore the blade from his jacket, which Runa had given

him. The iron was warm, almost alive, etched with words he didn't understand but felt in his bones. The weapon steadied him, its presence a thin line of calm against the chaos pressing in from all sides.

He ran.

Not away.

Toward her.

Toward the thing that had stolen her breath and buried it beneath the marsh.

The thing wearing Eira's skin stepped aside. She wasn't fighting him, not anymore. She was watching.

Waiting.

Zak drove the blade forward.

She caught it in her hand. The iron seared her palm, and she screamed—a sound that tore through the air, shredding the mist and sending the shapes behind her reeling.

The ground beneath them quaked.

The marsh cracked open wider, revealing not mud but glass.

A mirror.

The same mirror he had watched her vanish into.

The same mirror she had reopened from the other side.

The thing wearing Eira's skin threw him back. Zak hit the ground hard; the air was knocked out of him.

Above him, the mirror pulsed.

And through it, something began to crawl.

Not her.

Not Eira.

The thing that had waited too long, trapped between breaths and memory.

The Mother.

Not flesh. Not spirit. A hunger shaped like a tide, a presence that had forgotten how to be human.

Zak dragged himself to his feet. The blade still burned in his grip. He wasn't enough—he'd known that from the start.

The thing wearing Eira's skin stepped aside. She wasn't fighting him anymore. She was watching.

Waiting.

Zak took a step toward the mirror.

And then another.

The air thickened around him, pressing against his skin, pulling him forward like a riptide.

He reached the glass.

He pressed the blade against its surface.

The Mother opened one gleaming eye.

A voice spoke, not in the air or his mind, but in the marrow of his bones:

Come home.

Zak plunged the blade into the mirror.

The world buckled.

The Earth screamed.

And for a single, blinding moment, he saw her again.

Not the thing wearing her skin. Not the echo.

Eira.

Her hand reached for his.

He grabbed it.

The glass shattered inward.

And the salt flats collapsed.

The last thing Zak felt was her hand in his—not pulling him in, not letting him go.

Just holding.

The sea took them both.

And the sky above the Earth opened its mouth and wept.

Chapter Fourteen: The Hollow That Knows Her Name

The road twisted ahead, a black ribbon unfurling into the unknown. Zak drove slowly, his grip firm but steady, as though the car were an extension of his own hesitation. The world outside the windshield felt wrong—too still and heavy, as if the air resisted their passage.

Eira sat beside him, a quiet presence that filled the car more than her slight frame should allow. She stared out the window, her eyes tracking the skeletal trees as they blurred past. Her reflection in the glass was faint, almost ghostly, as though she were only half there.

Zak cleared his throat. "Do you remember how we got here?"

She didn't look at him. "I remember the parts that don't make sense."

Her voice was soft, almost distant, as if she were speaking to herself. Zak didn't press. He knew what she meant. The last few hours—or had it been days?—had blurred into a haze of half-remembered turns, flickering streetlights, and roads that seemed to shift when he wasn't looking.

"We're almost there," he said, more to himself than to her.

She turned then, her gaze meeting his for the first time since they'd left the motel. "It's not about where we're going, Zak.

It's about what's been following us."

He didn't answer right away. The truth sat heavy in the space between them, a truth he didn't want to name. "I thought we lost it."

Eira's laugh barely rose above the hum of the engine—dry, humorless, like it came from somewhere deep and hollow. "You don't lose something like that. It doesn't work that way."

Zak's fingers tapped the steering wheel, a nervous rhythm he couldn't quite stop. "Then what do we do?"

She leaned back, her hoodie slipping down to reveal the tangled mess of her hair. "We keep moving. Until we can't."

The motel appeared suddenly as though it had been waiting for them. Its neon sign sputtered in the twilight, the word "VACANCY" flickering like a dying breath. The building seemed to huddle against the encroaching darkness, its walls stained with salt and time.

Zak pulled into the lot, gravel crunching beneath the tires. He cut the engine, and the silence that followed was suffocating. Eira didn't move; her eyes were fixed on the mirror hanging just inside the doorway. It reflected nothing but the empty hallway behind them, yet it felt alive, watching.

"Did it follow us?" he asked, his voice barely louder than the quiet.

She hesitated. "No. It was already here."

The motel room was small and suffocating. Two narrow beds, a single flickering lamp, and a mirror seemed to dominate the space. The mirror didn't belong; its surface was too clean and perfect. It reflected nothing but the room's emptiness, yet it felt like it was waiting for something.

Eira paused at the threshold, her hand hovering over the doorframe. For a moment, Zak thought she wouldn't cross.

Then, with a quiet resolve, she stepped inside. The air seemed to shift around her as though the room acknowledged her presence.

Zak set her bag on the bed, his movements slow and deliberate. "Did it follow us?" he asked again, though he already knew the answer.

"No," she said, her voice barely audible. "It was waiting."

* * *

The air in the room felt heavy, charged with something unspoken. Zak couldn't relieve himself of the feeling that they were no longer alone, that something unimaginable had followed them, lurking just beyond the edges of their perception.

Eira sat on the edge of the bed, her posture rigid, her eyes never leaving the mirror. Zak watched her, trying to read the expression on her face, but it was like trying to catch smoke. She was slipping away, piece by piece, and he didn't know how to bring her back.

"We'll figure this out," he said, more to himself than to her.

She didn't respond, but he saw her fingers tighten around the edge of the bedspread.

The room was silent, but it wasn't empty. Something lingered there, something that had been waiting for them. Zak could feel it in the air, the way the walls pressed in around them.

He sat on the bed opposite her, careful not to move too quickly, as though any sudden movement might shatter the fragile balance. "We'll figure this out," he said again, his voice steadier.

125

Eira looked at him then, her eyes clear and sharp. "I know."

But the words felt hollow, and they both knew it.

The mirror fogged suddenly, a thin layer of condensation spreading across its surface. Eira stiffened, her gaze locked on the glass. Zak felt his pulse quicken, his throat tightening.

"What is that?" he asked.

She didn't answer. The fog thickened, curling through the room slowly and deliberately as if something behind it was testing the boundary—trying to find the right angle to break through.

Then came the sound.

Not sudden, not sharp. Just a long, low groan—like the hull of a forgotten ship shifting under the weight of memory. It echoed not from the mirror but from some deeper fold in the room, someplace beyond its walls, beyond what should have been real.

Eira rose slowly. Her movements were deliberate and trance-like, and her hand lifted toward the mirror with the caution of someone remembering a dream in real time.

"Eira—don't," Zak said, his voice tight, strained with something closer to dread than fear.

But she didn't stop. Her fingertips met the glass, and the surface rippled—not like a reflection, but like water stirred from the inside.

The cold came next. It pressed in from every side, a dense, airless weight that filled the room and hollowed out the sound. Zak tried to move and step forward, but his limbs wouldn't obey. Something held him there—not physically, but undeniably.

The mirror began to glow faintly, and then the figure emerged.

It wasn't her.

It was a child.

She was young, no more than nine or ten, with pale skin and hair that hung in wet, tangled ropes. Her eyes were too large for her face, black and endless, and her mouth moved soundlessly as though she were trying to form words that no longer existed.

"You remember me," the child said, her voice a soft, haunting melody.

Eira's hand dropped to her side. "I buried you in salt."

"You buried the wrong name."

The mirror cracked, a jagged line splitting the glass from top to bottom. Zak flinched, expecting it to shatter, but it held. The crack remained, a fissure in the surface that seemed to pulse with a life of its own.

Eira stepped back, her face pale. She didn't speak, didn't move. She stood there, her eyes locked on the mirror, as though she were seeing something Zak couldn't.

The child's voice came again, soft and insistent. "You remember me."

Eira's lips moved, but no sound came out.

The child's face wavered, and then, with a soft exhale, the mirror went dark.

Zak let out a breath he didn't realize he'd been holding. The room felt heavier now, the air thicker, as though the very walls were pressing in on them.

Eira turned to him, her expression unreadable. "It's not over," she said.

Zak nodded, his throat dry. "I know."

The air in the room seemed to vibrate with an unseen energy, and Zak couldn't shake the feeling that they were running out of time.

Chapter Fifteen: The Shape That Followed Her In

The room had grown too quiet.

Eira didn't announce her retreat. She moved slowly as if every step peeled her further from the world she and Zak had briefly shared in silence. With one last glance toward him—a glance he didn't see—she slipped into the bathroom, shutting the door without sound. She didn't reach for the light. The shadows were more honest than the bulb's artificial flicker.

She sat on the rim of the tub, her fingers tracing the cool porcelain, and then, as though answering something unspoken within her, she slid down into it, still clothed, knees drawn up beneath her chin. The enamel felt oddly pliant against her back, as if time had worn it thin. Her breath fogged the cracked mirror above the sink, the same one she'd touched earlier, the same one that had breathed back.

Runa.

The name left her lips like a thread unwinding: a memory, a wound, a call.

The mirror didn't reply—not directly. But the air shifted, dense and damp, and the steady drip from the faucet stretched, elongated, slowed to something less than time. A film-coated the edges of her awareness, and the walls seemed farther than they had moments before.

When she opened her eyes again, she wasn't sure she'd closed them.

The mirror was no longer above the sink. It had moved—or perhaps the room had reshaped itself around her. It stood directly across from the tub, tall, seamless, and unbroken by cracks. Its glass held no proper reflection. Instead, it shimmered with a murky opalescence, as if filled with the memory of light rather than light itself.

Eira blinked. The girl within the mirror did not.

She pushed herself upright, her fingers trembling against the curved edge of the tub. Her limbs responded, but the air pressed close, thick like saltwater. Movement felt earned, not given.

The figure in the mirror mirrored nothing. It sat, reclined, watching, but did not mimic.

"Where am I?" Eira whispered, the words forming clouds in the stale air.

A ripple disturbed the mirror's surface like a breath across a still pond. Then, without sound, it showed her a glimpse of the motel she'd left behind. Zak's belongings were still scattered on the bed. Her notebook lay open, and the pages were slightly curled. The lamp continued its feeble flicker.

The version of her was still curled in the tub.

She touched her face. Warm. Solid. Still hers. And yet the reflection stood now, its gaze locking with hers.

"You shouldn't have looked," the figure said.

The voice came from behind her.

She turned, heart skittering, but there was nothing. Just tile slick with condensation and shadows that didn't belong.

She stood slowly. As she stepped from the tub, the floor beneath her shifted. What should've been ceramic tile gave way to something denser, granular—packed salt and fine grit, the kind you only find in caves that have never known sunlight.

The room breathed. Not with air. With memory.

Light fled without warning. Not extinguished—banished. In its absence, something older stirred.

The mirror pulsed once—a recognition.

And then came the song.

Wordless. Melancholy. A woman's voice—low, fractured with grief. Familiar, though she couldn't place from where. She followed the sound.

***

The bathroom was gone—or had never existed. The walls she passed were slick and organic, pulsing gently beneath her fingertips. Ancient and imperfect spirals were etched into the stone. The air reeked of brine, damp ash, and earth overturned.

She moved forward, barefoot and unhesitating, not because she was unafraid but because the pull was stronger than her fear.

This was the Hollow.

It did not begin or end. It wasn't a place but an accumulation of memory, sorrow, blood, and longing. The Hollow was where forgotten names went to remember themselves, where echoes became whole. It held no sky because it had never needed one. Its ceiling was stitched with darkness, its floors folded with the bones of moments that had never found closure.

Each breath she took tasted of salt and ash, but beneath it

was something older still—a sweetness, like decay softened by time.

The corridor bent sharply, not because of stone or structure but because memory refused to move forward. And she understood, without being told, that this space fed on choices, on the gravity of half-made decisions and roads not taken. Each step forward was a negotiation with her mind.

She reached a vast, echoing chamber curved like the inside of a ribcage. Light came from no source she could name, but the walls shimmered faintly with a pearlescent sheen as though the Hollow remembered moonlight.

At the center: a pool, so still it gave the illusion of depthless air. Beyond it, a mirror. Not glass. Not metal. It was polished memory, a surface shaped by the weight of what had been lost and cracked, veined like the interior of a fossil.

She stepped forward. Her face stared back—older, heavier. Her eyes were darker, shadowed by things she hadn't yet lived.

"You're not lost," the reflection said.

Her throat constricted. "Then what am I?"

"A door. One that remembers when it was locked."

The wind stirred behind her. No air. No source. Just pressure—like the shifting of a great tide.

Within the mirror, Zak.

Kneeling. Broken. Cradling the stone.

She placed her hand on the mirror. It resisted, then gave slightly. A heartbeat later, it pressed back—out of sync, oppositional, as though it, too, was considering its next move.

"I want to go to him," she whispered.

"You will."

"But I'm afraid."

"So was she."

"Who?"

The mirror darkened. And then: a child on the shore, cradling a bundle in sealskin. The sea behind her was black with mourning.

A gust tore across the chamber. The mirror split. A jagged wound from top to bottom.

Pain bloomed in her hand. She looked down. Blood. A thin line across her palm. The spiral on her wrist glowed, lines tracing up her arm, the pattern alive with soft, pulsing heat.

The pool stirred.

It didn't ripple. It rose.

And from its edge, two women emerged—not walking, but forming. One from kelp and watertight, her robe glinting with barnacles. The other was tall, limned with smoke and brittle salt bone.

"You carry too much," said the smaller one.

"And too little," said the taller.

Eira didn't ask who they were. They felt like warnings. Or memories returned to check their weight.

"What is this place?" she asked.

"The Hollow," said the sea-woman. "Where silence remembers what voices forget."

"Where time is a wound," said the other.

"What waits beyond the mirror?"

"Truth," they said.

"Or what's left of it."

Her hands trembled. Her skin seemed to forget its shape. The lines shifted, faded, re-formed.

"I don't know who I am anymore."

"You've always known," said the taller woman. "But knowing isn't the same as remembering."

They stepped back, fading as though they had never been more than a thought pressed too hard into the world.

The pool was calm now. Expectant.

Eira stepped forward. Her blood painted the rim. Her breath caught.

Zak's name rose inside her. Not spoken. Remembered.

She stepped into the water.

And the Hollow took her.

She did not sink. She descended.

Not into water, but into memory so dense it had become substance.

And in that descent, she let go.

Not of herself.

Of everything that wasn't true.

Chapter Sixteen: A Face Made of Silence

The Hollow had no sky, but it pulsed with a rhythm that suggested breath. Not the rise and fall of lungs—but something older, something beneath the architecture of bodies. Respiration of worlds. Every beat stretched the space wider as if reality was held in a womb and someone—something was preparing to be born.

Eira stood at the edge of herself, or rather, at the edge of the version of herself that had now taken shape before her. The girl who wore her face—eyes missing, sockets brimming with black glisten like wet obsidian- stood inches away, her feet making no impression on the memory-wrought ground. Her skin shimmered faintly, as though light couldn't decide if it should reflect off her or be consumed by her entirely.

"You are not me," Eira said, but even as the words left her, they rang thin and fragile.

The figure smiled. Not with lips—those had begun to crack at the corners, drawn too tight, like parchment held too close to flame—but with presence. It was the kind of grin that lived behind the teeth, in the marrow of the thing that wore it.

"I am what is left of you," it said. "When you stopped turning away."

Eira's hands curled into fists at her sides. She could feel the Hollow pulsing through her fingertips now, around her and within her. It had begun to echo in her thoughts, not words, but in sensations—memories not her own, drifting through her mind like seaweed brushing skin in black water.

"Zak is here," she whispered, not to the thing, but to herself.

The figure nodded slowly. "Yes. He came for you. They always do."

"And you'll try to take him."

"No," the creature said. "You will."

The words hit like a slap beneath the ribs. Eira stepped backward, her heart hammering against the cage of her chest, but the mirror-Her stepped with her, mimicking not in gesture but in gravity—anchored to her every move.

"I'm not yours to control," Eira said. "This body, this blood—"

"Was never only yours," the figure hissed. "You carry the tongue of the first daughter in your breath. You speak of the sea without knowing. You call to the dead without mercy."

"I carry memory," Eira corrected. "Not obligation."

But the creature only tilted its head, and behind her, the Hollow began to whisper again—voices—hundreds, maybe thousands—layered and indistinct, like a crowd remembering itself.

Eira turned away from the figure and ran.

The Hollow changed underfoot with every step. What had once been a corridor of reflections now cracked apart into vast plains of shattered bone-glass. Each shard she passed reflected versions of herself she had not yet lived—one reaching through iron bars, another chained to a table, a third lying beneath a sea that pulsed with breath but no life.

The pain in her wrist flared. The spiral etched into her

skin moved again, the fourth arm curling inward with slow, deliberate hunger.

Behind her, footsteps echoed—not Zak's. Hers. The thing that wore her. The echo that had waited lifetimes to become flesh.

She stumbled into a clearing, and a monolith of bone stood at its center.

It rose impossibly high, pulsing with runes that bled red light across the surface like veins. In its reflection, the Hollow did not distort—it clarified. The endless churning of possibility stilled momentarily, and the mirror showed her a single truth.

Zak.

He was kneeling. Bruised. Bleeding from one ear. Holding the stone, the woman had given him, now cracked in two.

And behind him, rising like steam from a grave, came the first form of the Hollow. It did not walk. It unfolded. The limbs are too long. A spine that sang. A mouth that did not open so much as split.

Eira reached for the mirror, pressing both palms to the bone-slick surface.

"Let me through," she said.

The mirror pulsed once.

Then again.

And then it spoke—not aloud, but with the full body of memory:

"You are not whole enough."

Eira clenched her teeth. Her voice rose—not angry, not afraid, but commanding.

"Then take what you need from me. If it brings me to him."

The ground beneath her feet answered.

It cracked.

It opened.

And from the split rose a sound that did not belong in this world—like the ocean learning how to weep.

Eira screamed—but not in fear.

In offering.

The spiral on her chest unraveled.

She fell.

***

Zak saw her in a blink.

The Hollow tore open like wet cloth, and there she was—descending not from above but from the space between moments. Her body arced like a comet—lightless, breathless—before landing in front of him in a crouch.

Her eyes locked with his.

She was Eira.

And she was not.

"What did you give?" he asked hoarsely.

She didn't answer.

But the Hollow behind her froze.

And then, for the first time, it bowed.

Not deeply. Not like a servant.

Like a god meeting its reflection.

Zak reached out to her. "What did you give?"

Eira looked back at him, tears streaking her face—not from pain, but from weight.

"Everything that wasn't true."

Eira rose from the crouch in one unbroken motion, her body strangely fluid, as though the air around her had learned to accommodate her movement rather than resist it. Something had shifted in the curve of her spine, in the way her shadow no longer mirrored her precisely but moved half a breath behind. The Hollow recognized her now, not as prey or visitor, but as something grafted to its root—an inheritor.

Zak's breath caught in his throat. The sight of her—so near, so changed—was both relief and rupture. His instincts screamed to pull her into his arms, to test if she was still warm, still breathing, still his. But something older, deeper, more frightened whispered a warning: the thing that had returned to him might still be choosing who she was.

"What happened to you in there?" he asked, barely above a whisper.

Her eyes, too bright yet somehow hollowed, flicked toward him, then back to the bone mirror that had sealed behind her like a closing wound.

"I remembered," she said.

He took a hesitant step forward. "Remembered what?"

Eira's lips parted, but no sound came. The Hollow responded instead. All around them, the landscape began to shimmer—structures unraveling into the fog, walls pulsing into mist as if the place was losing cohesion in her presence.

Not dissolving. Yielding.

"I remembered what they did to her," Eira finally said. "The first one. The child in the mountain. They didn't seal her away to protect the world. They sealed her to stop the world from remembering her name."

Zak looked around, disoriented. "What do you mean?"

Eira walked toward him. Each step she took made the Hollow twitch—corridors folded, doorways recoiled, shards of broken memory stilled into silence. "The Hollow is not a prison. It's a wound. A memory scabbed over so many times it forgot how to bleed."

She stood before him now, the spiral on her wrist dim but thrumming with heat. He could feel it like a second heartbeat, syncopated with his own.

Zak reached for her hand, uncertain.

She let him take it.

It was warm. Human.

And yet, when he touched her palm, images flashed through him—fragments of something vast and buried: an altar slick with brine, voices whispering through rock, a baby's cry swallowed by waves, a triskelion etched into the ribs of a dying god.

His knees buckled.

She caught him.

"It's too much," he gasped.

"It has to be," she said gently. "The Hollow only opens for those who carry what it remembers."

He looked up into her face, no longer a girl's. There was something ancient in her posture now, in the stillness she held like a blade.

"Are you coming back with me?" he asked, the words brittle with hope.

Eira's gaze flicked skyward, though there was no sky, only breathless dark stitched with flickering lights that did not belong to stars. Her expression dimmed.

"I don't know," she said.

Zak stood slowly, eyes locked on her. "Then I'm not leaving without you."

Before she could respond, the air changed.

The Hollow shuddered violently, and a sound peeled across

the space from far behind them like thunder cracking through bone.

A new fracture.

A new arrival.

Eira's breath hitched.

"No," she whispered. "It's too soon."

Zak turned. "What is it?"

From the far corridor, a figure approached—slow, measured steps, but with gravity behind each one, like the very world reshaped to allow their passage. They wore no face—not obscured—absent as if the same concept of identity had been stripped from them.

The spiral on Eira's wrist turned black.

"The Hollow has made a choice," she said.

Zak stared at the figure. "What is that?"

"The memory of the first," Eira murmured. Given shape. The thing that should have died when the gate first closed."

The wind of the Hollow kicked up, howling without direction. Around them, the bone mirror cracked again.

The figure extended a hand.

Not in welcome.

In demand.

"You have to choose," Zak said, voice breaking.

Eira turned back to him, tears forming in her eyes.

"I already did. I gave everything that wasn't true."

Then she pressed something into his palm—a smooth stone, cool and veined with red.

"What's this?"

"The way out."

He shook his head. "Not without you."

But she was already turning, stepping into the path of the

faceless figure. The Hollow narrowed around her like a throat.

"Eira!" Zak shouted, but the name fell heavy, swallowed before it echoed.

She looked back one last time.

Not as the girl who had stepped into the mirror.

But as the one who had survived it.

Then the light flared—

And she was gone.

V

Part Five: Through the Vein of the Forgotten

Something followed her back, but not in footsteps.
It came through in the pauses. In the weight of her
name. In this way, mirrors hesitate now before
showing her face.
The institution called it recovery.
She knows better.
She was never meant to return.
And the world she came back to already knows that.

Chapter Seventeen: Salith'anor

The word had once tasted like smoke and salt on her tongue—foreign, fragile, a shape she hadn't understood but had known deep in her blood. Salith'anor. She had whispered it as if repeating something heard in a dream, unaware it was not a name but an invitation. A summons. A remembering.

Now, that word bloomed in her like marrow turned to fire.

In the Hollow's heart, where even light seemed to bend in reverence, Eira stood before a wall etched with the ancient script—spirals, slashes, and circular runes that pulsed not with ink but intention. Her voice, hoarse from her passage, broke the silence.

"Salith'anor," she said again, not whispered this time, but declared.

And the Hollow answered.

Not with words. With weight.

The ground beneath her feet throbbed. The walls contracted. From the arch above, a thread of memory spilled—a scene she had never lived and yet recalled too vividly. A woman, robed in sea-colored wool, stood over a newborn cradled in a bowl of salt. The word passed from her lips like benediction. Salith'anor. The voice of the beginning. The first breath before breath.

And in that moment, Eira understood.

It was not a spell. It was a lock.

It was the word meant to keep the Hollow asleep.

And she had spoken it aloud.

Spoken it into the light.

Spoken it into ruin.

The ruin did not collapse with violence or scream; it unfolded slowly, deliberately, like the moment before a wave breaks—full of pressure, aching to release. The Hollow, vast and coiled in silence, did not shatter when she named it. It expanded. It remembered. And in remembering, it began to gather its scattered pieces, not with fury but with inevitability.

Eira's knees buckled as its weight crashed into her—not as an impact, but as a knowing. The kind that coils behind the eyes and presses against the ribs from within. The word she had spoken wasn't a key or a curse or a prayer. It had always been a door. And she had stepped through it by saying it aloud, not once but again and again in her dreams, her memories, her breath—each time believing she was merely repeating something old instead of becoming something ancient.

She collapsed to the floor of the Hollow, the ground shifting beneath her like the stretched hide of some slumbering beast, not beating with life—but with memory. The walls around her, once disguised as corridors, peeled back and vanished, giving way to an open, roofless void. There was no sky above, only a vast sweep of layered recollection—like smoke frozen in resin, swirling in slow, deliberate folds. And there, at the center of it all, the triskelion turned—not carved or drawn, but alive, breathing, spinning in rhythm with the air itself.

"Salith'anor," she whispered again, not out of ritual now, but out of recognition.

And the Hollow exhaled in reply, not with air, but with time.

The air shimmered like heat rising from stone, and within that shimmer, a shape emerged. At first, she thought it a reflection—an echo of herself drawn thin—but it held itself with too much stillness and weight. It had no face, no eyes, no voice, but somehow it watched her. And the moment it appeared, the burning in her wrist intensified until it felt like her skin might split and spill the truth it had tried to contain.

She pressed her hand to her chest as if to steady something breaking open beneath her sternum, but the world around her was no longer consistent. The Hollow blurred at the edges, flickering between its own form and the shape of something else—something she knew too well and not at all.

And then, it changed.

It wasn't the Hollow anymore.

It was linoleum under her feet. Cold. Slick. Sterile.

The scent of bleach and old plastic invaded her lungs, and the hum of distant fluorescent lights buzzed faintly above her head. She knew this sound. Knew it too well. The hiss of an automated door closing. The soft clink of a tray being slid beneath a locked opening. And just like that, the Hollow had receded—not entirely, but enough. Enough to let the world pull her back.

She was in Saint Amaranth.

Or rather, she was lodged beneath it. Through it. Echoing across its sterile walls with the weight of the Hollow still in her bones.

She staggered back from the sink and caught her reflection in the brushed steel panel above the faucet. It shouldn't have reflected anything, and yet it did. Her eyes met her own—but it was the her from the Hollow. The one that didn't blink. The one that smiled when she didn't. The one that remembered her name not as Eira, but as something older, unspoken.

The nurse's voice drifted in from the hallway beyond the door.

"She's quieter today. Staring again."

Another voice, lower: "She'll come back. They all do."

But Eira hadn't left.

She had simply been split.

Time cracked at the edges, and for a moment, she saw them all: the Runa kneeling before the altar of bone; the girl who had drowned but never died; the woman she might become, standing barefoot at the mouth of a new world, hair tangled with kelp and eyes darkened by knowing. Each of them whispered back to her, not in language but in rhythm. Salith'anor. The first word. The final invitation.

She pressed her hand to the steel again, and the reflection stilled. No movement. No mimicry.

And then—

A shadow behind her.

Not in the room.

In the mirror.

Zak.

His silhouette was faint and trembling, as though trying to break through glass that wasn't glass. His mouth moved, but no sound came. Only the look in his eyes reached her. Recognition. Fear. And something deeper. Devotion.

Her lips moved before she could think to stop them. "I remember."

The mirror flared with light—bright enough to bleach the corners of the room and hot enough to melt the air from her lungs. The nurse opened the door at that exact moment, startled by the static surge and flickering lights.

"Miss Vardalok?"

But Eira was already falling backward.

Not physically.

Through time.

* * *

Back in the Hollow, Zak clutched the broken stone the woman had pressed into his palm—now glowing violently, each crack pulsing in rhythm with Eira's fading presence. He could feel her slipping, not away from the Hollow, but deeper into something worse: forgetfulness. Detachment. The kind of severing that left you alive, but not whole.

He had reached the altar stone, the same one Eira had collapsed against, and he pressed his forehead to its cold surface. He didn't cry. He didn't scream. He breathed, and in that breath, he said her name—not as it had been written on forms or whispered in prayer, but as it had sounded the first time he knew he was already too far gone to leave her behind.

"Come back," he whispered. "Not for me. For you."

And somewhere—either in the Hollow or beneath flickering fluorescent lights—her heart answered.

Not with a word.

But with a knock.

Once.

Twice.

A pause.

Then a third.

Chapter Eighteen: Beneath the Room That Breathes

Time had not passed in the Hollow; it had simply pooled like water in the basin of a stone, and now it drained with a slow inevitability. Eira lay on her side; one cheek pressed against the altar stone, it's surface cool and slick with condensation. Her breath moved in shallow waves, curling like fog around her lips as if uncertain whether it belonged in this place or elsewhere. Light flickered across her closed eyelids in stuttering pulses, though when she opened her eyes, there was no discernible source—only the rhythmic beating of something unseen, a memory she couldn't place yet felt inexorably tied to her.

She sat up slowly, her fingers splayed across the altar as if anchoring herself against a tide that only she could sense. The silence that had once enveloped the Hollow was replaced by a trembling tension, as though the air itself had become a fragile fabric, stretched taut by something trying to break through. Across the glade, the Hollow seemed to twist in on itself, its edges fraying, revealing something beneath its surface.

A figure stood there, tall and imposing, robed in black that seemed woven from midnight itself. Its face was hidden beneath a veil of ash and thread, concealing any features. It did not speak, nor did it move. It simply waited, as though it had all the time in the world.

Eira rose to her feet. Her limbs felt heavier, as though her body had become an anchor she had to drag with her. The spiral etched into her wrist, which had been still moments before, now darkened at its center, as though drawing inward, hungry for something she couldn't name. She stepped toward the figure, each step heavier than the last, as the world around her began to fragment.

The trees around her bled into columns, and the stone beneath her feet shattered into tiles. The Hollow itself seemed to peel back, dissolving into something else—something familiar and yet foreign. She recognized it, even as it resisted recognition: Saint Amaranth. The institution's presence seeped through the Hollow like a haunting, its bed rails, clipboards, and locked doors flickering in and out of existence, as if the boundary between the two worlds was thinning.

The figure turned to her, its veil falling away, revealing a face that was both strange and familiar. It was her own face, but older, worn by time and experience. Her future self, perhaps—sunken eyes steady, hair streaked with white, lips cracked but unflinching.

"You remember now," the figure said, though the voice was not spoken aloud. It vibrated through Eira, as though it came from within her own mind. "But you do not yet believe."

Eira didn't respond, her eyes fixed on the figure before her. "Am I meant to become you?" she asked, her voice barely a whisper.

"You already are," the figure replied. "But you may still choose which memory of you survives."

Before Eira could respond, the Hollow trembled violently,

as though something had torn through its fabric. She felt the tear, a sensation that was both physical and emotional, as if the world itself was unraveling.

Zak stood in the Hollow's final corridor, the broken stone clenched in his fist pulsing with a light so bright it threatened to blind him. The walls around him cracked, not from any external force but from a resistance within, as though something sacred was finally surrendering to a force it could no longer contain.

He was close now. He could feel it. Her name echoed in his mind, a mantra that grew louder with each step.

Eira. Eira. Eira.

He moved forward, his breath ragged, his hands shaking. The Hollow pressed in on him from all sides, but for the first time, it did not resist. It watched him, measured him, as though it, too, was waiting for something.

And then he saw her. She was not standing but falling, tumbling through light and time, her body moving as though pulled by an unseen current. He caught her mid-collapse, her weight falling against him, her eyes wet but unwavering.

"I saw myself," she whispered, her voice muffled against his shoulder.

"I know," he replied, his voice steady. "So did I."

He helped her to her feet, his arm wrapped tight around her ribs. She was thinner now, more fragile, as though the journey had taken something from her. But when she looked at him, her gaze was clear, sharp, awake.

"I think I'm forgetting," she said, her voice trembling. "The more I remember, the less I know what's real."

Zak didn't answer. He simply held her, his grip firm, as though he could anchor her to him, to this moment, to whatever reality they were in.

The corridor groaned around them, and from behind them came a new sound—footsteps. But they were not human. They were heavy, uneven, wet. Whatever had been waiting in the Hollow, the thing Eira's name had called forth, was moving. And it was following them.

***

They did not run. There was no point; the Hollow had no geography, no direction to escape to. Movement here was not about distance but resolve. And so they walked, their steps slow and deliberate, as the walls around them began to close in.

"I don't think it wants to devour me," Eira said, her voice taut. "It wants to wear me."

Zak's jaw tightened. "Then it'll have to tear through me first."

Eira didn't respond, but her hand slid into his, squeezing tightly. "It already has," she said, her voice barely a whisper.

The corridor grew colder, the walls slick with condensation that wasn't moisture but memory made visible. Faces surfaced in the stone, half-formed and unblinking, their mouths slightly open, as though caught mid-confession. Each face bore her features, distorted, like echoes of a melody played too many times.

"I remember being every one of them," she murmured.

Zak reached out, his hand touching the nearest wall. The face beneath his palm exhaled, a soft mist forming on the surface. He recoiled, but Eira didn't move. She watched as the wall smoothed over, as though nothing had disturbed it.

"I think I've been here before," she continued, her voice

distant. "Maybe not me. But someone like me. Someone who looked into the Hollow and didn't blink fast enough."

The corridor narrowed ahead, sloping downward in a spiral that felt less like a structure and more like the vertebrae of some ancient, buried creature. They descended slowly, neither speaking, both aware of the weight of what lay ahead. Around them, the walls began to hum, a low, mournful sound, like voices too old to remember how to form words.

At the center of the spiral, the passage opened into a vast, spherical chamber. Suspended in the air, as though caught between moments, was a mirror. It was not framed, not tethered, not supported by anything. It simply hovered, its surface darker than glass, shimmering like water before a storm. It reflected nothing, yet seemed to hold everything.

Eira knew, without knowing how that this was what the Hollow had been guiding her toward. This was the cradle of all remembrance, where names were etched in perpetuity.

Zak stepped forward, but the chamber resisted him. The moment his foot crossed the threshold, a wave of nausea struck him, and the floor seemed to buckle beneath him, throwing him backward.

Eira caught his wrist before he could fall. "You can't follow me in," she said, her voice flat, inevitable.

Zak nodded, his jaw clenched. "I'll wait," he said.

"You always do," she replied, and then she stepped forward, crossing into the chamber.

The mirror accepted her. It didn't ripple or shine; it breathed as though it were alive. She stood before it, watching as, one by one, her selves appeared—the girl she had been, the child who had whispered to the shadows, the teenager who had run, the woman who had opened the corridor. And behind them all, barely distinguishable, another version of herself.

Runa. Not a reflection but a memory woven into the blood that now pulsed visibly beneath her skin.

The spiral on her wrist began to rotate, a slow, deliberate movement, like a gear turning.

"I remember the gate," she whispered. "I remember the child. I remember the promise."

The mirror shuddered, and from within it, a voice spoke—her voice, but older, steadier. "You are the bridge, not the barrier. The mouth, not the seal."

Eira stepped forward, and the mirror swallowed her.

Zak didn't wake; he returned and slammed back into his body as though reality had rethreaded itself around him. His breath caught in his throat, sharp and painful. The Hollow was gone.

He lay sprawled in the rain, outside the ruins of a chapel. The stone he had carried was gone, his hands empty, the scar on his palm faint and healing. The fog moved slowly across the field, heavy and silent.

He sat up, gasping, his body aching. She was gone. Not dead, but changed. He could feel it.

He reached into his coat and pulled out the folded piece of paper—a map with the name Saint Amaranth circled twice. A place he had once thought was an institution. Now, it was a direction.

He stood, his legs unsteady, and began to walk toward the road. Toward her. Toward whatever had come back wearing her name.

Eira opened her eyes in a bed that smelled of bleach and paper. The institution's ceiling blinked down at her, its fluorescent lights flickering. The Hollow, deep within her,

listened.
Waiting.
Still open.

Chapter Nineteen: Stillness Has a Voice

The first thing she noticed wasn't her own breathing but the hum of the fluorescent lights overhead—a low, insectile pitch that belonged to places claiming order but never quite achieving it. The hum wasn't steady; it faltered occasionally, as though the current itself wavered, unsure of its purpose.

Then came the cold.

It wasn't sharp or biting but a slow, pervasive chill that seeped from the cinderblock walls and vinyl floors. It was a sterile kind of cold, stripped of warmth or memory, carried by air that had been processed too many times through metal vents. The faint tang of bleach mingled with something older, something that lingered in the corners of the room.

She blinked, her eyelids dry, as though they hadn't closed in days.

Above her, the ceiling stretched, off-white fading to beige, marred by a single hairline crack that traced its way toward a buzzing vent. She knew this ceiling, not for its color or design but for the hollow it conjured within her—a void she had felt the first time she had stared up at it and realized she no longer recognized herself.

Saint Amaranth.

She was back.

Her body felt heavy, uncooperative. The mattress beneath her was stiff, covered in crinkling plastic, and her blanket smelled of industrial detergent—clean but lifeless. Her fingers, pale and faintly bruised at the knuckles, rested on top of the sheet. A paper wristband encircled one arm, its edges curling from the moisture in her skin.

The spiral was gone.

There was no scar, no ink, no trace of the mark that had once carved itself into her flesh. And yet, something remained—a resonance, a faint thrum beneath her skin, like a frequency just beyond hearing.

She sat up slowly, the room around her holding its breath. It wasn't silent, not truly. Outside the door, carts rattled, voices murmured, and a television droned in a distant common room. But here, in this room, sound felt muffled, as though it, too, had been medicated into submission.

They had found her two days ago.

Unconscious.

Curled at the edge of a rain-soaked field, barefoot and shivering. Her clothes had been torn, a smear of blood at her temple with no wound beneath it. No signs of assault. No explanation for how she had come to be there. Locals called it exposure. Paramedics suspected hypothermia. Doctors at the emergency room found no drugs in her system, no injuries to explain her state. Just a girl without a name who wouldn't wake when they called her.

When she finally stirred, they sent her here. To Saint Amaranth.

Because sometimes, when a person doesn't wake the way

the world expects, the world puts them in a box. Padded walls. Curved furniture. Locked doors.

Catatonia, the chart had said.

Not because she was frozen, unmoving. But because when she did wake, she didn't speak. She didn't flinch. She didn't ask where she was. She simply opened her eyes and stared at the ceiling as though she could see something moving beneath the plaster.

And in truth, she could.

Eira swung her legs over the side of the bed. The floor was cool linoleum, its surface scuffed from years of carts and shuffling feet. Her balance wavered, but she stayed upright. Above the sink, a mirror hung—brushed metal, warped enough to distort her reflection but not enough to hide the stillness in her eyes.

She walked to it and stared.

Her reflection stared back.

But it wasn't quite her.

She was paler than she remembered, her hair limp and uneven. Her cheekbones looked sharper, her skin stretched tight over them. There was a stillness to her now, not calm or controlled, but a quiet like the surface of water before it ripples.

Her hand hovered in front of the mirror.

Then she whispered, "Salith'anor."

The light flickered.

The sink groaned.

And for a fraction of a second, her reflection didn't move.

It stared back at her, blinking half a beat too late, as though it belonged to another rhythm entirely. It wasn't malicious, wasn't mocking. Just... off.

Eira stepped back, retreating to the chair by the wall.

Let them come, she thought. They always did.

The nurse arrived first—young, with neat braids and a clipboard she didn't look up from until she was halfway through her questions. Eira didn't answer. Not because she couldn't, but because their questions weren't the right ones. How are you feeling today? Do you know where you are? Do you remember what happened?

She ate a little. Crackers. Toast. A few slices of apple. She ignored the overcooked meat and the pudding sealed in foil. The food wasn't real. It was an idea of food, designed to sustain without satisfying.

Night in the institution wasn't dark. It was blue—a soft, artificial glow meant to calm, though it only made her skin feel thinner, as though the light could seep through her pores. She lay flat on her back, eyes open, staring at the ceiling. She wondered if the vent still led somewhere or if it simply recirculated the same air, over and over, until it no longer belonged to anyone.

That's when she felt it again.

Not loud. Not sudden.

Just there.

A shift in the pressure behind the walls. A creak that didn't belong to the building's bones. A movement that wasn't tied to pipes or ducts or anything that belonged to the living.

She rose slowly, crossing the room to the sink.

The mirror had fogged slightly, as though something on the other side was breathing.

And in that fog, a handprint had appeared.

The fingers were too long, spaced too wide. A faint spiral marked the center of the palm.

She didn't touch it. Not yet.

Instead, she pressed her hand to the tile below the sink, where the cold seeped into her skin. Beneath it, she felt something—a rhythm, faint but steady.

A pulse.

Not mechanical. Not human. Not a memory.

A tether.

* * *

The next morning, two doctors came.

The younger one spoke first, his voice too bright, too rehearsed. He was trying to connect, to humanize himself. But he didn't see her. He saw a patient, a case, a problem to be solved. The older one hung back, watching quietly until something in her eyes shifted.

Then he stepped forward, laying a photograph on the bed.

Stone steps, weathered by time. A jagged cliff. A spiral carved into a standing stone, its edges softened by sea and wind.

She looked at it.

She didn't know how, but she knew this place.

"I've been there," she said.

The old doctor didn't look surprised.

In group therapy, she sat silent, watching the others speak in circles about fears that looped back on themselves. But one woman—frail, with skin like chalk—spoke of a corridor made of mirrors, of a girl in a crown of brine, of words she could almost remember but couldn't form.

Their eyes met.

Recognition passed between them.

Eira stood.

"Would you like to share?" the therapist asked.

"No," she said.

She left.

No one stopped her.

Back in her room, the mirror waited. It was no longer fogged, no longer a mirror at all. It shimmered, pulsed, as though something on the other side was pressing against it.

And in its depths, something smiled—not with malice, but with memory.

She didn't remember walking to the corner of the room.

She simply was there, folded into the wall as though she had always belonged to it. The floor was cold beneath her hands. Beneath the tile, the pulse thrummed again, stronger now.

A whisper threaded through the walls, soft and insistent. Fingers brushed against concrete. A presence that wasn't coming—it was already here.

Her breath slowed.

Her eyes closed.

And behind them, something began to open.

The next morning, Eira woke to the sound of footsteps outside her door. A soft knock came moments later, and a nurse poked her head in.

"Good morning," the nurse said, her voice too cheerful, too rehearsed. "How did you sleep?"

Eira didn't answer. She didn't see the point. Sleep wasn't something she had done—not truly. She had closed her eyes, and the world had shifted around her, but it wasn't rest. It was something else.

The nurse didn't seem to expect a response. She bustled in, clipboard in hand, and began taking stock of the room, checking off boxes on her list. "You have a visitor later this morning," she said, her tone bright and falsely reassuring. "Someone from administration."

Eira didn't respond. A visitor. She wondered what kind of visitor came to a place like this, where the walls seemed to absorb more than they reflected.

After the nurse left, Eira rose from the bed. She moved through the morning routine mechanically—washing her face, brushing her hair, changing into clean clothes that didn't feel entirely clean. The fabric was stiff, as though it had been laundered too many times, stripped of any softness it might once have had.

Breakfast was the same as every other morning—bland eggs, toast that crumbled at the touch, and a carton of juice that tasted more like sugar than fruit. She ate quietly, watching the others in the common room. Some sat listlessly, staring at nothing. Others chattered to themselves or to invisible companions. A few cast furtive glances her way, as though trying to decide if she was someone worth noticing.

She ignored them all.

After breakfast, she returned to her room. The mirror above the sink was clear now, no trace of the fog from the night before. She stared at her reflection, searching for something—anything—that might explain the creeping unease that had settled in her bones.

There was nothing.

The morning dragged on. Eira sat in the common room, ignoring the television that flickered in the corner, its sound muted. She watched the people instead—the nurses bustling back and forth, the patients wandering aimlessly, the doctors who swept through with their charts and their questions, as though any of it mattered.

She was so lost in her own thoughts that she didn't notice the administrator's arrival until a shadow fell across her.

"Eira?"

She looked up. The administrator—a woman in a crisp suit, her hair pulled back into a tight bun—stood before her, a clipboard tucked under one arm. Her expression was polite but detached, her eyes scanning Eira as though she were another item on a checklist.

"I'm here to discuss your discharge," the administrator said.

Eira blinked. Discharge. The word felt foreign, as though it belonged to another language.

"You'll be leaving us tomorrow," the administrator continued, her tone practiced and smooth. "Your paperwork is nearly complete, and we've arranged for a release back into society into a arranged living arrangement. It's a quiet place, with more freedom. A step toward reintegration."

Eira stared at her, unmoving. Reintegration. The word felt hollow, meaningless.

"Do you have any questions?" the administrator asked, her smile never quite reaching her eyes.

Eira shook her head. Questions. She had so many, but none that this woman could answer.

"Very well. We'll go over the details with you later today. For now, just relax. You'll be out of here before you know it."

The administrator walked away, her heels clicking against the linoleum. Eira watched her go, feeling something in her chest tighten.

She would be discharged. Again.

She wasn't sure if the thought filled her with relief or dread.

The rest of the day passed in a blur. Eira moved through the motions—group therapy, lunch, another round of questioning from a nurse who didn't really want to hear her answers. The news of her discharge hung over her like a weight, pressing down with every passing moment.

That night, she lay awake in her bed, staring at the ceiling. The low buzz of the fluorescent lights felt louder now, more insistent. She could feel the pulse beneath the walls, faint but steady, as though something was calling to her.

She closed her eyes, trying to quiet her mind, but the whispers were there, just beyond hearing. They threaded through her thoughts, soft and insistent, pulling her toward something she couldn't quite see.

When she finally slept, her dreams were fractured—fragments of places she couldn't quite remember, voices she couldn't quite understand. She walked through corridors that twisted and turned, their walls lined with mirrors that reflected nothing but darkness.

She woke with a start, her heart pounding. The room was dark, the blue glow of night seeping through the small window high on the wall. For a moment, she wasn't sure where she was. Then the familiarity of the room settled over her, and she remembered.

Saint Amaranth.

She would be discharged tomorrow.

The thought should have brought her comfort, but instead, it left her cold.

She didn't belong here, but she wasn't sure she belonged out there, either.

The next morning came too soon. Eira moved through the motions of getting ready, her mind elsewhere. The administrator returned, this time with a stack of paperwork and a small bag of belongings that had been taken from her when she arrived.

"Everything is in order," the administrator said, her tone brisk and efficient. "You'll be leaving after lunch. The transfer team will meet you at the front entrance."

Eira nodded, taking the bag. Her belongings felt foreign, as though they belonged to someone else.

She spent the next few hours in a daze, her thoughts drifting. She didn't speak to anyone, didn't engage with the nurses or the other patients. She simply waited.

After lunch, a nurse came to escort her to the front entrance. Eira followed, her steps slow and deliberate. The hallway seemed longer than she remembered, the haunting ceiling lights overhead flickering slightly.

At the entrance, a small group of people waited—orderlies, a driver, and a man in a suit who introduced himself as her caseworker.

"Eira," he said, extending a hand. "I'm here to help you with the transition, and have you well on your way to a normal life. We'll get you settled in your new accommodations."

She looked at him, his hand still extended, and didn't move.

He lowered his hand awkwardly, his smile faltering. "Right. Well, let's get going."

They led her outside, into the cool afternoon air. A van waited, its engine idling. Eira paused, taking a deep breath. The air tasted different here—crisp, with a hint of something sharp and metallic.

She climbed into the van, her movements mechanical. The door slid shut behind her, and the vehicle pulled away, carrying her toward whatever came next.

As the institution faded into the distance, Eira stared out the window, watching the world go by. The trees blurred past, their branches bare and skeletal. The sky was a flat, gray expanse, heavy with unshed rain.

She didn't know where she was going.

But she knew one thing.

She wasn't free.

Not yet.

They said she was leaving. But something else was arriving.

Chapter Twenty: The Quiet Thing That Followed

The van moved with numb predictability, its tires humming low against the cracked asphalt of a back road that seemed to stretch endlessly into a horizon Eira couldn't quite decipher. The rain had begun to mist around the windows, thin trails of water slipping down the glass-like veins, obscuring the world beyond into shifting patches of gray and movement. She didn't ask where they were going, and no one offered the answer. The caseworker beside her—middle-aged, clean-cut, with a voice that probably did better in courtrooms or bureaucratic offices—glanced at her once or twice, unsure whether to make conversation. But the look in Eira's eyes made his decision for him.

She sat with her hands folded loosely in her lap, fingers cold but steady, and her gaze locked not on any one thing outside the window but on the vague sensation of movement itself, like her body was being ferried between two halves of a life she still hadn't decided to claim. Every so often, a low patch of fog would roll across the road, and for a moment it would seem like the van wasn't moving at all, just suspended in place, trapped in a corridor between moments. And that, somehow, felt closer to the truth.

They passed an abandoned gas station; its roof collapsed in one corner, and the sign above rusted into illegibility. A playground with no children. A junkyard dotted with pale blue tarps that trembled under the wind. The buildings grew fewer. The trees pressed closer. And with each mile, the air thickened—not just with the weight of rain, but with that same ache Eira had come to know as the Hollow's signature: not a sound, not a smell, not a visible mark, but a pressure, a sense that something unseen had turned its attention toward her and never looked away.

She shifted slightly in her seat, one hand resting on the edge of her coat pocket where the discharge papers still sat folded and unread. There was something absurd about it—a list of medications she didn't take, a follow-up appointment she would never attend, a name printed in bold that she'd stopped feeling connected to weeks ago. It felt like an obituary written too early.

"Not much longer now," the caseworker said finally, as though he'd rehearsed the phrase for the last twenty minutes and had just now found the courage to speak.

Eira didn't respond.

The van turned onto a gravel road that wound through a dense copse of pine and maple, their wet branches arching overhead like a canopy of skeletal arms. Somewhere in the distance, a bird cried out—a sharp, guttural sound that didn't quite match anything she remembered from childhood. She tried not to look directly into the woods. The trees were too still. Too deliberate. Like they were waiting for something.

Eventually, the road opened to a clearing, and there it was: the house. It was not a facility, not a hospital, just a long-forgotten schoolhouse converted into something resembling a home. The wood was weather-worn, the paint stripped in places to reveal gray slats beneath. The porch sagged slightly at one end. The windows were dark, blank, and watching.

The van came to a stop.

The driver killed the engine.

Neither man moved to open the door for her. They didn't need to. Eira knew this was where the instructions ended. From here, she was supposed to begin whatever came next.

She stepped out into the wet afternoon, boots sinking slightly into the soft gravel. The air was colder and sharper here, and the rain had become more deliberate—no longer mist but pinpricks of cold collecting on her hair and lashes. She pulled her coat tighter around her shoulders and approached the house slowly, each step feeling heavier than the last.

The caseworker followed at a distance, duffel bag in hand.

"There's a key under the porch," he said. "Your name's on the lease. Groceries are stocked. You'll have someone check in every few days. But mostly, you're on your own."

She looked at him then—really looked—and saw how deeply uncomfortable he was, how badly he wanted to be back in his van and headed toward paved roads and fluorescent offices. Whatever lay beyond this clearing was not a world he wanted any part of.

"Thank you," she said, and her voice didn't sound like her own. It was quiet. Distant. Like someone else had said, it came through her mouth.

He nodded once and left the duffel by the steps.

When the van reversed down the long gravel path and finally disappeared around the bend, the silence that followed was not empty. It was full—dense, like water pressing in on all sides. Eira stood a moment longer beneath the overhang, staring at the door. She didn't feel fear, not exactly. But there was a gravity here, a pull that settled into her spine and said: whatever waits inside, it knows you've come.

She retrieved the key and opened the door.

The scent hit her first—old wood, cedar, something faintly antiseptic. The air inside was warmer than she expected, though untouched, like the house had been waiting in a kind of suspended animation. The layout was simple: one large central room with a worn couch, a table, and shelves mostly empty. A narrow hallway led off to a kitchen and two bedrooms. A mirror above the fireplace was old and cloudy.

She moved through the space slowly, fingertips brushing the edges of furniture, the doorframes, the shelves—as though trying to anchor herself to the physicality of it, to remind herself that she was still here, still tangible. The spiral had not returned to her wrist. But it hadn't left either.

She set her bag on the bed in the smaller room and stood there for a while, staring at it. Then she moved back to the living room, past the fireplace, and paused before the mirror.

Her reflection stared back.

Tired. Thinner. But still hers.

Almost.

She lifted her hand to the glass. Didn't touch it. Just held it there.

"I'm here," she whispered.

Nothing happened.

Not right away.

That night, the house did not sleep. It shifted, settled, and moaned with the slow breath of old foundations adjusting to the presence of something new. She lay on the bed, staring at the ceiling, listening.

At 3:14 a.m., she woke.

Not startled.

Summoned.

The mirror in the living room was no longer cloudy. It gleamed, not with light, but with attention.

She rose, bare feet on cold wood.

Each step a heartbeat.

And when she stood before the it, she didn't speak.

She didn't have to.

Because someone else did.

"Elin," said the voice from the glass.

And Eira remembered everything.

The cliff. The circle. The stone that bled without cracking. The whisper that wasn't a word but a door.

And she knew.

She wasn't done.

Not even close.

* * *

The next morning arrived not with sunlight, but with the same dull gray hush that had hung over the property since she arrived. The sky, smeared in tones of pewter and ash, pressed low against the hills, as if trying to smother the earth beneath it. Eira hadn't slept much, though she had closed her eyes, listening instead to the restless sounds of the house: the beams groaning under their own weight, the faint, rhythmic pulse of the mirror that no longer showed her anything at all, and something beneath the floorboards that dragged its unseen limbs just out of reach.

She didn't unpack. She couldn't bring herself to. Every object in her duffel bag felt wrong in her hands as if she were trying to arrange pieces in a dollhouse that belonged to someone else's life. Instead, she paced the length of the small house with slow, deliberate steps, taking inventory not of her belongings but of how the air seemed to shift depending on which room she entered. The kitchen felt watchful, as though it were waiting for something to happen. The living room held its breath, tense and still. The hallway near the second bedroom—the one she hadn't yet opened—whispered faintly, as though voices lingered just beyond hearing.

At midday, a car pulled into the gravel driveway. Eira didn't flinch at the sound of tires crunching over stone. She stood at the window, watching as Zak stepped out of the car. He slung his jacket over one shoulder and carried a grocery bag in his hand, his eyes scanning the porch and window and finally finding her. He didn't wave. When she opened the door, he stood there for a moment, silent, holding the bag between them like a peace offering.

"You look better," he said, his voice low, almost hesitant.

She stepped aside to let him in. Zak glanced around as he entered, his boots leaving flecks of gravel on the hardwood floor. "Still smells like a basement, but at least it's dry. That's something."

"Why this place?" she asked, her voice tired rather than accusatory.

He set the groceries on the counter. "Called in a favor."

"From who?"

Zak hesitated, cracking the seal on a bottle of water before answering. "You remember I mentioned a guy named Lars? That guy from the circle in Oslo County? He has family up this way. They keep a few off-grid spots for… situations like this. Places with no paper trail. Places people forget."

Eira looked toward the mirror above the fireplace, its surface dull and lifeless. "And you thought bringing me to one of those places was a good idea."

Zak leaned against the counter, his voice steady. "I thought it was the only place that wouldn't be afraid of you."

She let his words hang between them, heavy and sharp.

After a while, she murmured, "They said I was catatonic. But it wasn't like that. I wasn't gone. I was stuck. I saw everything— the fields, the sky, the way the walls turned to mouths."

Zak didn't interrupt, letting her speak.

"And I felt it," she continued, her fingers brushing the inside of her wrist. "Still feel it. It didn't leave me."

He stepped closer, his voice quieter now. "It never would."

They sat together on the old couch, their silence stretching like a taut wire. Eventually, Zak pulled a folded piece of paper from his coat pocket and held it out to her.

"I found this under the floorboards of your room in Glencrest," he said. "Didn't open it. Thought maybe it was for you."

Eira unfolded the paper carefully. The handwriting was hers, or close enough to be unsettling. It read: When the girl with no name finds the door again, she must not speak the word aloud. There was no signature, only a single spiral drawn at the bottom of the page.

She read it twice, then pressed the page flat on the table. "I didn't write this."

"I was afraid of that," Zak said quietly.

Rain began to fall harder outside, sheets of water blurring the treeline and drumming against the roof. Eira stood and walked toward the hallway, her steps slow but deliberate, toward a room she hadn't opened.

"You're going in there?" Zak asked, his voice tinged with concern.

"I have to," she replied.

The second bedroom door opened without resistance. The room was dim and empty, with a chair in the far corner, an old child's desk, and a broken standing mirror propped against the wall. The glass was cracked down the center, but unlike the others, this one showed a reflection, not of the room but of something else entirely.

A cliff. A standing stone. The sea. And at the edge, a girl with hair tangled by the wind.

"That's not possible," Zak whispered from behind her.

"It's not a mirror," Eira said, her voice steady. "It's a window."

Outside, the wind rose to a howl, rattling the windows and shaking the walls. The spiral on her wrist flared, invisible but present, and something beneath the floorboards vibrated with a soft hum, like stone singing through water.

She turned to Zak. "It followed me here. Or maybe I followed it."

Before he could respond, a low creaking groan echoed from beneath the floorboards, followed by a heavy thud. It wasn't the sound of a house settling—it was the sound of something arriving.

Zak crossed the room in two strides, pulling her back from it. "We need to go then!"

"No," she said firmly. "We need to listen."

A gust of wind slammed against the house, and the lights flickered. She could see the girl at the cliff's edge turned around. She wasn't Eira. She wasn't Elin. She was someone older, or younger, or neither. She wore the crown of brine, her eyes carved in runes, and when she opened her mouth, the spiral on Eira's wrist pulsed in response.

Zak backed away, his voice strained. "Who the hell is that now?"

Eira didn't move. She stared at the figure in the mirror, unwavering.

The girl raised her hand and pointed directly at them. Not a threat. A summons.

The glass cracked wider, its surface glowing faintly. The floor shuddered beneath their feet.

And just before the room split into shadow and light, Eira spoke the word she wasn't supposed to utter again: "Salith'anor."

It didn't shatter. Instead, it opened, its surface rolling tides like water as the air hummed with old soul energy. The space beyond stretched into an endless, swirling expanse, where reality blurred into a dream, and the faint scent of salt and damp earth filled the air.

Zak hesitated, his grip on her arm tightening. But Eira leaned forward, her eyes fixed on the threshold—the spiral on her wrist burned amber orange, a silent beacon guiding her forward.

Through the glass, she saw them.

Runa stood at the shoreline, face lifted to a wind that didn't reach this world, her eyes searching like she'd been waiting all this time.

Varg stood just behind her, silent and fixed, the same grim stillness she remembered from the Hollow—watching her.

They weren't gone. They'd just been waiting for her to come back.

* * *

Beneath the collapsed chapel at Glencrest, the earth had split clean to the bedrock.

Ava was not missing.

Not anymore.

In the dark, something sat with her now. Not a woman. Not a child. Just limbs in the wrong order and a mouth that hadn't yet decided how to smile.

Elin stood at the edge of the broken foundation, barefoot, hair soaked with sea-mist that hadn't touched the air above.

She didn't blink.

The thing that wore Ava's skin turned its head slowly—bone cracking, face slack—and whispered a word that had never belonged on land.

Elin whispered it back.

And the Hollow welcomed them home.

Appendix: The Codex of Salt and Shadow

Recovered from fragments hidden beneath the skerry graves, translated by unknown hands...

The Runes of the Saltblood Line

These ancient sigils predate ink and fire. They were carved into stone, bone, and blood. Some say they were whispered into the world by the old gods themselves, carried on salt winds.

Below are nine of the known runes tied to the Saltblood legacy:

Fehu — The Brand of Beginning

Wealth, luck, sacrifice

Fehu marks the first trade of life for power. Among the Saltblood, it is burned into the palm of those who are chosen— those fated to pay in blood.

Raido — The Path Between Worlds

Journey, rhythm, cycles

This rune was often drawn beside mirrors or waterways. It signifies movement not only through space, but between realities.

Hagalaz — The Breaker

Destruction, storm, uncontrollable forces

Often found near sites of unnatural death or weather anomalies. The Saltblood elders say this rune breaks what must be broken to rebuild.

Algiz — The Watcher's Mark

Protection, sight, higher awareness

Carved into stone thresholds and worn as amulets, it is believed to allow the bearer to see what others cannot — but at a cost.

Dagaz — The Divide

Daybreak, transformation, irreversible change

Dagaz signals the moment before waking — or dying. In Saltblood lore, it is the rune of the mirrored self.

The Nine-Wound Path

A ritual known only to the eldest Seiðr priestesses. Each rune cut into the flesh becomes a wound through which the past may speak. No one who has walked the path has ever returned unchanged.

* * *

RUNA, SKY-HEWN AND UNCLAIMED

- **Known As:** Wound-Singer, Blade-Daughter of the Marsh Moon
- **Apparent Age:** Twenty winters, though her eyes remember stars before fire

"The wind faltered when she arrived. It has never recovered."

Runa does not carry time; she unthreads it. Born under a moon too close and too red, her breath was the first thing to stir the drowned stones of Skelvik in a hundred years. The salt rose when she cried. Mirrors dulled. Birds flew backward.

She did not learn the runes — they whispered themselves into her skin. **Hagalaz**, the unmaker, pulses just below her collarbone. It hums when something is about to end.

Her blade was forged where sky struck sea — an edge found

in a thunderclap, not a forge. It sings when she moves. She never walks anywhere twice.

She left without leaving. Her name lingers in the reflection of water just before it turns dark.

VARG, THE SALTED GOD

- **Epithets:** The Hollow-Eyed King, First Warden of the Bound Threshold
- **Form:** Weathered into shape by war and wave — vast, firelit, never mortal

"To look into his eyes was to meet your oldest fear — and it knew your name."

Varg is a myth scraped from stone and dragged through ash. He did not rise. He surfaced. The fjords remember his weight. When he walks, wolves go silent. When he stills, the air presses in like it knows better.

There is a mark over his heart — not ink, not burn, but something older. **Algiz**. The rune of the sentinel. The rune of those who do not blink.

He stood at the ninth seal when it cracked. Legends say he uttered a single word, and the mountain behind him bowed.

He is not dead. He is not waiting. He is what the gate fears will return.

ELIN, CLOAKED-WALKER AND FLAME UNSEEN

- **Called:** The Quiet Bloom, She Who Threads the Unmaking
- **Aspect:** Pale as breath in winter, shaped like a girl, heavier than fate

"She is the pause between a question and its answer — when your heart forgets what it meant to say."

Elin is not seen; she is felt — a pull in the gut, a shift in shadow, the echo of something not yet done. She did not step through the mirror. She became the seam.

She leaves no rune behind, but they coil in her speech. Glass fogs where she lingers. Candles betray their flame to her. Clocks wind in reverse.

She once shared laughter with Runa, though none remember the sound. Her presence tastes like rain before it falls.

If you meet her, you already did.

She doesn't ask questions. She is what you become when you stop answering.

The Salt-Tongue Verses
Fragments carved into stone, passed through flame and brine.

"What Was Written Beneath the First Stone"
No blood was spilled, yet the land drank deep.
A mark was carved, not with hand, but with grief.
It was not made to bind — only to be known.
And what knows cannot forget.

"Oath of the Ninth Door"
I stood before the last door sealed in salt,
Where no god dared knock, nor ghost return.
One step forward and the breath is not your own.
One step back, and nothing ever was.

"Elin's Lament Before the Fold"
She watched without seeing, heard without breath.
Threaded through memory like fog through bone.
Her name is not hers. It is silence recalled.
Speak it, and the air forgets your voice.

"The Blade Dreamed in Salt"
They say it fell from a sky that never was.
They say it wept when it first drank blood.
They say it sings — but only before ruin.
The blade has no master, only memory.

"For Those Who Cross the Mirror"
You left something behind.

It walks now, in your shape.
You will meet it again.

It has not forgiven you.

Conclusion

She knows now: not everything can be named, and not all truths wear faces.
Some wounds don't scar—they echo.
Some paths don't circle back—they open.
What happened here can't be retold. It can only be felt.
Not every ending is closure.
Some endings are inherited.
And this—
This was never a story meant to end.

Only one meant to awaken.

— *Ophelia Fey*

Epilogue

***

It didn't return through the front door.

There was no creaking floorboard, no shattering mirror, no wind howling through the trees like some ancient omen. Just a stillness—so profound, so complete—it didn't feel like silence at all. It felt like replacement. Like the world had been quietly folded inside-out and laid flat again with something new stitched just beneath the surface.

Eira lay in bed with her eyes closed, but her body already knew what her mind hadn't yet spoken aloud: something had changed. Not arrived—changed. The Hollow didn't need to be open to reach her anymore. It never truly had. It wasn't a place, not in the way rooms or roads were places. It was rhythm. Memory. Invitation. And now, it was inside the walls again. Not as a monster clawing through the cracks—but as something subtler, older. Something that remembered her name even when she had forgotten her own.

Downstairs, Zak slept in the threadbare armchair, one boot still on, a knife tucked beneath his jacket and salt crusting the windowsill where he'd laid it out like a prayer. He hadn't stirred when the air shifted. Hadn't noticed how the house had begun to breathe differently, deeper, as though it were making room for something long exiled.

But Eira had felt it the moment the mirror disappeared. The moment the spiral on her wrist pulsed and didn't fade. Since the voice that wore her own face called her "daughter." Since the salt in her blood had started to hum like the sea whispering to a tide that had always, inevitably, returned.

Outside, the woods no longer whispered—they listened. Each branch bent slightly inward, every leaf turned toward the house like ears tilted to catch a forgotten word. Inside, the cold had changed texture—it wasn't biting, it wasn't painful. It was reverent. It was recognition.

And then, the floor beneath her bed warmed—just once, a single thud like a heartbeat pressed into the foundation.

A shadow gathered in the doorway. Not cast. Not shaped. Gathered.

Elin.

Not fully here. Not fully gone. But closer than memory.

She didn't speak. She didn't move. She didn't have to.

Time, slippery and strange, had begun folding inward again, each crease tighter, sharper, more deliberate. It wasn't unraveling this time. It was aligning.

Eira opened her eyes. Slowly. Without fear. Without surprise.

She looked toward the doorway, and the shadow that waited there like a question she'd already answered. Her pulse didn't quicken, but the spiral on her wrist throbbed once, then again, in steady rhythm with something deep below the floorboards.

This wasn't aftermath.

This wasn't survival.

This was the beginning of what had been waiting.

And in the stillness that followed—so full it felt like the house had swallowed sound itself—came a new noise:

A low hum, like breath drawn in through stone.

From the baseboards. From the fireplace. From the very walls.

And then a voice—not hers, not Zak's, not Elin's—rose from beneath the house and said,

"You left the gate open."

Afterword

Dear Reader,

Reaching the end of a book—whether you've written it or lived inside it—is always a strange thing. There's a kind of silence that follows. Not emptiness, exactly—just stillness. A pause before the next thing begins.

Thank you for reading this one. For staying with it. For following wherever it needed to go.

This story built itself slowly. I didn't always know where it was headed—only that it insisted on being written. Page by page, it revealed what it wanted to become. I'm grateful you chose to walk alongside it, especially through the quiet, the strange, and the parts that refused easy explanation.

If something in these pages felt familiar, unsettling, or unshakable—I hope you carry it with you. Not as an answer, but as something worth returning to.

There's more ahead. I'm already writing it.

With all my thanks,

—Ophelia Fey

About the Author

Ophelia Fey holds a degree in anthropology and has spent years investigating paranormal phenomena across forgotten towns, wooded hollows, and spaces that slip between maps. Her work draws deeply from a lifelong fascination with belief systems, inherited memory, and the fragile threshold between personal experience and the unknowable.

With a background steeped in folklore, trauma research, and fieldwork rooted in the strange and the liminal, Ophelia crafts fiction that lingers in quiet rooms and speaks in the space between thoughts. Her stories explore identity, silence, and the long shadows cast by the things we carry—especially the ones we don't talk about.

She writes for those who've ever felt a pull toward something unnamed, those who believe some truths haunt rather than reveal, and anyone who's ever wondered if memory can echo across bloodlines.

Saltblood is her debut novel and the first in a continuing series.

She writes what lingers when everything else is quiet.

To learn more, visit www.theopheliafey.com

You can connect with me on:

🌐 http://www.theopheliafey.com

Also by Ophelia Fey

Saltblood: Born of Brine
The mirror didn't close behind her.

It opened something worse.

Eira crossed through, chasing the truth—but the Hollow followed. Now she and Zak live in a house that shifts when no one's watching, where mirrors stay too clear after dark, and salt gathers in the corners of the floorboards without wind.

They don't speak about what they saw.

But neither of them forgets.

In Glencrest, something is waking beneath the ruin.

Ava, the girl who vanished without a sound, is back

Or something wearing Ava's shape is.

She doesn't bleed. She doesn't blink. She speaks a name no one taught her.

And Elin is with her. Waiting. Feeding it stories.

What began as a fracture in the mirror is now a rip in reality.

And the Hollow doesn't need to pull them back in.

It's already here.

Born of the Brine

Book Two in the *Saltblood* Trilogy